HOT OFF

Although we're in the dead of winter, you wouldn't know it from the scorching chemistry between suave billionaire Case Fortune and a certain strawberry-blond heiress! The moment they locked eyes, sparks were flying like crazy. Gina Reynolds, the award-winning children's author, didn't exactly put up much resistance when the debonair tycoon set out to win her heart. And those two sure didn't waste any time hitting the sheets....

It doesn't take a psychic to forecast a high-society wedding for this red-hot duo. Hmmm... But perhaps there is more to this whirlwind love affair than meets the eye. Top-secret info leaked to us by an anonymous source suggests ... may be more enamored of acquiring Miss Reynolds' family business, Reynolds Refining, than he is of her. Tsk...tsk... The unsuspecting Miss Reynolds is probably too blinded by lust—or is that love?—to realize what her "doting" fiancé has up his custom-designed sleeve. And it probably has little to do with picking out china patterns.

In all likelihood, these white-picket promises are all part of Case's plot to make the filthy-rich Fortune clan even more formidable....

Dear Reader,

Welcome to the world of the Dakota Fortunes, the six-book continuity following the lives and loves of the Fortune family. You may recognize the last name of this family—they've been around for a long time in various forms, in various series, including Silhouette Desire. This particular branch are cousins to the Fortunes of Texas as well as the Australian Fortunes. In fact, you'll meet a few of the Australian cousins in these books.

I hope you enjoy this family, which has been fractured by the death of our patriarch's first wife and his bitter divorce to wife number two. But, as time progresses, you'll learn that it's Nash Fortune's third marriage that is really going to cause some scandals.

Now, sit back and enjoy *Merger of Fortunes,* the story of a willful Fortune male and the one surprising woman who is about to put him in his place.

Happy reading!

Melissa Jeglinski

Melissa Jeglinski
Senior Editor
Silhouette Books

Please address questions and book requests to:
Silhouette Reader Service
U.S.: 3010 Walden Ave., P.O. Box 1325, Buffalo, NY 14269
Canadian: P.O. Box 609, Fort Erie, Ont. L2A 5X3

PEGGY MORELAND

MERGER OF FORTUNES

Silhouette® Desire

Published by Silhouette Books
America's Publisher of Contemporary Romance

Special thanks and acknowledgment are given to Peggy Moreland for her contribution to the DAKOTA FORTUNES series.

To Kathy Combs and Mary Crawford, the two saps who were left out of the book I dedicated to my college buddies. You may have been overlooked, but will never be forgotten!

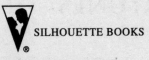

SILHOUETTE BOOKS
®

ISBN-13: 978-0-373-76771-7
ISBN-10:   0-373-76771-4

MERGER OF FORTUNES

Recent Books by Peggy Moreland

PEGGY MORELAND

published her first romance with Silhouette Books in 1989, and continues to delight readers with stories set in her home state of Texas. Peggy is winner of the National Readers' Choice Award, a nominee for the *Romantic Times BOOKreviews* Reviewers' Choice Award, and a two-time finalist for the prestigious RITA® Award. Her books frequently appear on the *USA TODAY* and Waldenbooks bestseller lists. When not writing, Peggy can usually be found outside, tending the cattle, goats and other critters on the ranch she shares with her husband. You may write to Peggy at P.O. Box 1099, Florence, TX 76527-1099, or e-mail her at peggy@peggymoreland.com.

THE DAKOTA FORTUNES

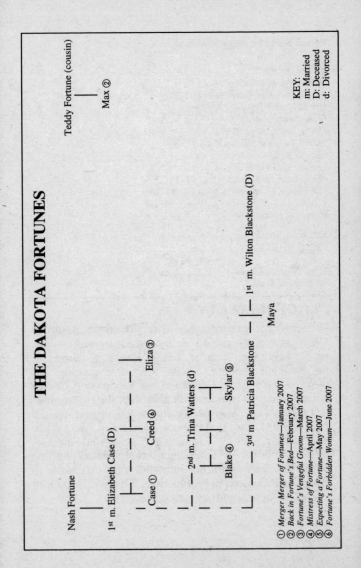

Nash Fortune

Teddy Fortune (cousin)
Max ②

1st m. Elizabeth Case (D)

Case ①   Creed ⑥   Eliza ③

2nd m. Trina Watters (d)

Blake ④   Skylar ⑤

3rd m Patricia Blackstone

Maya

1st m. Wilton Blackstone (D)

① *Merger Merger of Fortunes*—January 2007
② *Back in Fortune's Bed*—February 2007
③ *Fortune's Vengeful Groom*—March 2007
④ *Mistress of Fortune*—April 2007
⑤ *Expecting a Fortune*—May 2007
⑥ *Fortune's Forbidden Woman*—June 2007

KEY:
m: Married
D: Deceased
d: Divorced

One

"Well, I'll be damned," Case Fortune murmured in disbelief. He would've thought librarian-attire would be a pre-requisite for writing kids' books. Horn-rim glasses, sensible shoes, a dress that covered chin to ankle. That kind of thing.

He glanced up at the banner that stretched from one end of the bookstore's children's corner to the other to make sure he was at the right place: Signing Today! Gina Reynolds, Award-Winning Author of TALES FROM TOADSVILLE.

Toadsville, he thought, swallowing a laugh. What kind of woman wrote stories about toads? A nerd, he decided, and shifted his gaze back to the woman in question.

But Gina Reynolds didn't look like any nerd he'd ever seen before. At the moment she was perched on a child-size chair holding a book open, so the children scattered on the floor around her could see the illustrations as she read the story to them. Seated as she was, her legs appeared incredibly long, their length enhanced by the short black skirt that hit her above her knees and the black leather boots that came just short of reaching them.

Her style of dress wasn't the only contradiction to Case's preconceived image of Gina Reynolds. Long strawberry-blond hair framed her face and tumbled in soft waves over slender shoulders. A faint sprinkling of freckles speckled her nose. Her eyes, a stunning leaf-green, sparkled with animation as she read to the children in a voice that changed tone and depth to match the personality of the characters in the story.

Case hadn't come to the signing expecting to find a raving beauty—and he hadn't—yet there was something about her that encouraged a man to take a second look. Whether it was her physical attributes or her voice that demanded that second look, he wasn't sure, but the sound of her voice had him moving to brace a shoulder against the end of a bookshelf to listen, as enthralled as the children with her storytelling skills.

When she read the last page and closed the book, the children let out a collective sigh of disappointment, then immediately began clamoring for her to read another. A woman—probably the manager of the bookstore—quickly stepped into the circle of children to intervene.

"I'm sorry, children" she said, with regret, "but that's all the time Ms. Reynolds has to read to you today. If you'd like her to sign copies of your books, please form a line against the far wall." She turned to smile at Gina. "I know that Ms. Reynolds will be happy to personalize each one."

With surprising gracefulness, Gina rose and moved to sit behind the table set up for her, where stacks of her books were displayed. Children scrambled to form the requested line, which quickly stretched from one end of the store to the other.

Though irritated that he would have to wait a little longer to introduce himself, Case wasn't giving up. He needed Gina's assistance in bringing a merger to fruition, and wasn't leaving until he'd at least had the opportunity to discuss it with her. Seeking an inconspicuous spot, he slipped between the aisles of books and pretended to study the titles, while waiting for the kids to clear out.

When the last kid in line turned away, Case made his move. Quickly crossing to the table, he picked up a book from the display. "Would you mind autographing one for me?" he asked.

Bent over to gather her purse from beneath the table, she glanced up, a friendly smile ready. Though her smile remained in place, it lost some of its warmth when her gaze met his—and that surprised him. He didn't know her and was sure that she didn't know him, yet it was definitely dislike—or, at the very least, disapproval—that darkened her eyes.

Straightening, she accepted the book and laid it on the table in front of her. "And who would you like it inscribed to?" she asked as she flipped open the front cover.

"Case Fortune."

She glanced up in surprise. *"You?"*

"Is that a problem?"

Blushing, she quickly shook her head. "Of course not. It's just that…well, you're the first adult male who's ever requested an autographed book."

He shot her a wink. "I've always prided myself on being ahead of the curve."

Instead of the smile he'd thought his teasing comment would draw, he received a frown.

Bending her head over the open book, she scrawled an inscription, then closed the cover and handed it to him. "You pay the clerk at the register," she informed him curtly and reached for her purse again.

He nodded. "Thanks."

Before he could get to the real reason for his visit, the manager called from behind the checkout counter, "Ms. Reynolds? I'd like to speak with you before you leave."

"I'll be right there," she replied, then rose and said to Case, "If you'll excuse me."

Irritated by the obvious brush-off, Case pulled his wallet from his hip pocket and followed her to the front of the store. He tossed a credit card on the counter, but kept an ear cocked to the conversation transpiring between Gina and the manager, and overheard the woman congratulate Gina on receiving the Newbury Award. While he continued to listen, he noticed a photo on the wall behind the register of the woman with Gina. The plaque beneath it read "Susan Meyer, Manager."

After signing the credit slip and accepting his autographed book, he approached the two women.

"Ms. Meyer?" he asked hesitantly.

She glanced his way. "Yes. May I help you?"

He extended his hand. "Case Fortune."

Her eyes shot wide at the Fortune name. "Oh, Mr. Fortune," she gushed and pumped the offered hand enthusiastically. "It's an honor to have you in our store."

"The honor's mine," he said humbly. "I'm sorry to interrupt, but I couldn't help overhearing you say that Ms. Reynolds won the Newbury Medal. I'm not familiar with that award. Is it a prestigious one?"

She pressed a hand over her heart. "Oh my, yes! The American Library Association presents it to the author they feel has made the greatest contribution to American literature for children." She angled her head to smile fondly at Gina. "And this year they've chosen our Gina. We're all so proud of her accomplishment."

"I should think so," he agreed, then turned his attention fully on Gina. "I suppose you've been swamped with parties celebrating your success."

Color seeped into her cheeks. "Well, no. Not exactly."

"An oversight I hope you will allow me to rectify by permitting me to take you out for cocktails."

Her face went slack. *"Cocktails?"*

"It seems appropriate."

"Oh, no," she said, shaking her head. "I couldn't. I appreciate the invitation, I do, but I need to stay and help Susan clean up from the booksigning."

"You'll do no such thing," Susan fussed. "You're our guest. My staff and I will put everything away." She pushed out her hands, shooing the two toward the store's entrance. "Go and celebrate," she ordered Gina. "It's not everyday you have the opportunity to toast your success with such a handsome man."

Henri's, the restaurant Case had chosen for Gina's celebration, was not only located near the bookstore, it was reputed to be one of the finest in Sioux Falls, South Dakota. During the weekday, businessmen crowded the interior, networking while partaking in the infamous two-martini-lunch. In the evenings, it was no less busy, as many of those same businessmen returned to entertain their clients, plying them with pepper-crusted tenderloin or smoked salmon—Henri's signature entrees—accompanied with select wines from Henri's wine cellar. Friday and Saturday nights a different atmosphere prevailed, one created for couples seeking a quiet, romantic dinner. Gina knew this because her father had often brought her mother to Henri's on Saturday nights, a ploy he'd used to charm his way back into her good graces, after having ignored her all week. Many of his cronies did the same.

She stole a glance at Case, wondering if he used Henri's for that purpose. He wasn't married, thus had no wife to placate, but he had plenty of lady friends who might feel similarly slighted. She was aware of his bachelor status, as a week rarely passed that his picture didn't appear in the newspaper's society section, with a different woman on his arm each time. Trophy dates, eye candy. Whatever a person termed his choice in women, the man obviously didn't lack for female companionship.

So why had he insisted upon taking her out for

cocktails? she asked herself, studying him beneath her lashes. She didn't believe for a minute that it was because he wanted to toast her success. Men like Case Fortune did nothing that didn't benefit themselves in some way and he had nothing to gain from her winning an award.

Frowning, she continued to scrutinize him as he and the waiter went through the opening-the-champagne-bottle ritual. She hated to admit it, but he was better looking in person than in the photos she'd seen of him in the papers. Razor-cut, dark-brown hair; finely chiseled features. The leather jacket he'd draped over the back of his chair looked Italian, as did his tailored dress shirt. Probably were, she thought with more than a little resentment. He had the money, the style to wear whatever he wanted. Why settle for anything less than the best? Her father certainly never had.

The reminder of her father was enough to have her glancing at her wristwatch, wondering how long she'd have to stay before she could make a graceful exit. Five minutes? Ten?

"Your champagne, madam."

Startled, she glanced up to find the waiter offering her a flute of champagne. She forced a smile for his benefit and accepted the glass—all the while silently cursing the bookstore manager. With Susan all but pushing her out the door, there was no way she could've refused Case's invitation without appearing rude and ungrateful.

"To many more Newburys in your future."

She looked up to find that Case had his flute lifted in a toast. Murmuring a polite, "thank you," she took a cautious sip of champagne. She didn't particularly care for the bubbly beverage. It was her father's signature drink, reason enough for her to dislike it.

She shuddered at yet another reminder of her father and set the glass down, knowing Case was the one responsible for bringing him to mind.

He looked at her in concern. "If you don't care for the champagne, I can ask the waiter to bring you something else."

She shook her head. "Thanks, but I'm really not much of a drinker."

He nodded, then his expression turned curious. "You know, I'm surprised we haven't met before. Living in the same town, and all, you'd think our paths would have crossed at some point."

She lifted a shoulder. "No surprise, really. I went away to boarding school and college, and only returned to Sioux Falls a couple of years ago."

"I guess that explains it," he said, then smiled. "I do know your father, though. In fact, I'm one of his biggest fans. He's built Reynolds Refining into a force to be dealt with in the world marketplace. His company is both well managed and financially sound, which says a lot in today's economy."

Bored with the conversation, she looked away. "I wouldn't know," she said vaguely.

"You don't stay abreast of your father's business?"

"No."

"Why not?"

Rather than answer, she glanced at her watch again. "I really should go."

He lifted a brow in surprise. "But we haven't finished our champagne yet."

She laid her napkin on the table and gathered her coat. "Like I said, I'm not much of a drinker."

Bracing his arms on the table, he leaned to peer at her intently. "I get the distinct impression that you don't like me."

Embarrassed that she hadn't concealed her feelings better, she avoided his gaze as she pushed her arms through her coat sleeves. "Not you personally," she said uneasily. "Men like you."

"And what kind of man is that?"

Annoyed that he wouldn't let the subject drop, she grabbed her purse. "I really do need to go. Thank you for the champagne."

He placed a hand over hers, stopping her.

"I'd like to see you again."

His eyes were an incredible blue and fixed on hers with an intensity that she found difficult to look away from. "I-I don't go out much. My work takes most of my time."

"You have to eat, don't you?"

"I usually have my meals at my desk."

"May I at least call?"

She panicked for a moment, unable to think of a polite way to refuse, then rose, dragging her hand from his. "Sure," she said, and forced a smile. "Thanks again for the champagne."

Before he could say anything more to delay her, she turned and strode away.

Case Fortune wouldn't be calling her, she thought smugly. He couldn't.

Her phone number was unlisted.

"Have you made any progress with the Reynolds merger?"

Case reared back in his desk chair, stifling a sigh, as his brother Creed took a seat opposite his desk. Although he would've preferred his brother hadn't brought up what was turning out to be a sore subject with him, he couldn't really blame him for asking. It was Dakota Fortunes' money that was tied up in the purchase, and as co-President, a position he shared with Case, Creed had as large a stake as Case in the merger's outcome.

"No," he admitted reluctantly. "But I'm working on it."

Creed swore under his breath. "Dammit, Case. Do I need to remind you how much we've got riding on this merger?"

"I'm fully aware of what our investment. Can I help it if Reynolds has gone soft on the deal?"

Creed rose to pace, dragging a hand over his hair. "Surely there's a way to force his hand."

"I'm working on the daughter. She's the cog in the wheel. Reynolds has decided to leave the company to her, instead of selling it to us, as he'd agreed."

Creed stopped to peer at Case. "Daughter? I didn't know Curtis had any kids."

"Neither did I, until he told me he'd changed his mind about selling to us."

"Does she have any business experience?"

Case snorted a laugh. "Hardly. She's an author. Children's books, no less. As far as I can tell, she has no interest in the company at all."

"Then why does Reynolds want to leave it her? You know as well as I do how volatile the oil and gas industry can be. If she gets hold of the refinery, she'll bankrupt it in a month."

Case scowled, having already considered the probability. "You're not telling me anything I don't already know." He opened his hands. "But what can I do? Reynolds has decided he wants to leave it to her as a legacy of sorts."

"You're going to have to force his hand. Make him go through with the merger."

"I'm working on that," Case assured him. "The daughter's the key. It's just a matter of persuading her to convince her old man that she doesn't want the company."

"And how do you plan to do that?"

Case folded his hands behind his head, his expression cocky. "Don't worry, little brother. I know how to handle women."

Creed rolled his eyes. "Forgive me," he said, and turned for the door. "For a moment, I forgot who I was talking to."

When the door closed behind Creed, Case dropped his hands and frowned, the confident act no longer necessary. The truth was, he'd been blowing smoke when he'd told his brother he could handle women—at least, *this* particular woman.

How the hell was he going to persuade Reynolds' daughter to help him, when he couldn't even talk to her? he asked himself. The woman had outfoxed him. A nerdy writer of children's books had duped Case Fortune, a world-class negotiator.

He huffed a breath, as he recalled the innocent smile Gina had offered him when she'd given him permission to call. Hell, the woman had known damn good and well he wouldn't be able to call. Not when her phone number was unlisted.

Getting her number wouldn't be all that hard, he reminded himself. A few calls to the right people and he'd have the number quickly enough. But he couldn't chance obtaining it that way. The minute she heard his voice, she'd know he'd acquired her number by dubious means, which would give her even more reason to dislike him.

And she disliked him enough as it was. Or, rather, men like him, he remembered her saying. And what the hell did that mean, anyway? he asked himself in frustration. What kind of man did she think he was? Some kind of pervert?

He gave himself a shake. Didn't matter what kind of man she thought he was, it was obviously the *wrong* kind, and it was up to him to convince her differently.

But how?

A smile slowly spread across his face, the answer so obvious he was amazed he hadn't thought of it before. Stretching out a hand, he punched the intercom for his secretary.

"Yes, Mr. Fortune?"

"Marcia, call the florist and order three dozen yellow roses to be delivered to Gina Reynolds."

"Is her name in your personal or business database?"

"Neither. She's Curtis' daughter. You may have to dig a little to find her address. Have someone in legal check the county tax records. I'm sure she's listed there."

"Will do. How do you want the card signed?"

He considered a moment, then bit back a smile. "Toad lover."

"Excuse me?"

"Toad Lover," he repeated. "T-O-A-D. I assume you know how to spell lover."

"Uh, yes, sir, I do."

"And ask the florist if they can find a container shaped like a toad to put the roses in. Preferably crystal or silver."

"Whatever you say," she said, sounding doubtful. "Is this some kind of joke?"

"No. More like war."

The first time the doorbell rang, Gina ignored it. Perched on a stool before her drafting table, she was riding a creative wave, the images in her mind all but flowing off the end of her pencil. If she stopped now, the images might vaporize before she had the opportunity to commit them to paper.

The doorbell rang a second time and she hunched her shoulders against the intrusive sound, trying to block it out. The third time, she muttered an oath and slapped the pencil down. Prepared to hang and quarter the person who dared interrupt her work, she marched to the front door of her loft. Mindful of "safety first," she rose to her toes to peer through the peep hole.

And saw roses. Yellow roses. What appeared to be a field of them. Curious, she swung open the door and fell back a step, clapping a hand over her heart. "Oh, my word," she breathed, stunned by the sheer size of the arrangement that greeted her.

"Delivery for Ms. Gina Reynolds."

The male voice came from behind the roses and obviously belonged to the person holding them.

She strained to peer through the blooms. "I'm Gina."

"Where would you like me to put these?"

"I'll take them," she offered stretching out her hands.

She shifted left and right, down and up, searching for something to grip, but finally gave up.

"Maybe you better bring them inside," she conceded. "Hang on a minute and I'll guide you."

Stepping out into the hallway, she positioned herself behind the delivery boy and placed her hands on his shoulders. "Straight ahead," she instructed, then warned, "Careful. There's a large support column on your left. Good," she praised as he shifted slightly to the right and avoided bumping into it. "My dining table is directly in front of you. You can set the arrangement there."

Heaving a sigh of relief, the young man deposited the roses on the table, then pulled an invoice from his pocket. "Sign here," he said, pointing.

"Who are they from?" she asked curiously, scrawling her name.

The boy tucked the invoice back into his pocket. "Beats me. There's probably a card in there some place. Usually is. If not, you can call the shop. Somebody there will probably know."

Nodding, she drew a five dollar bill from her purse. "Thank you," she said. She handed him the tip, then eyed the arrangement dubiously and added, "I think."

After locking the door behind the delivery boy, she returned to the dining table and began searching for a card. Not finding one among the blooms, she squatted down to see if it was attached to the vase.

"Oh, my gosh," she cried, when she found herself staring into the jeweled eyes of a silver toad. Charmed by the intricately crafted creature, she spied the card and removed it, sure that she'd find her agent's name there, along with his congratulations on her receiving the Newbury Award.

"Toad Lover?" she read with a frown, straightening. She turned the card over and read the neatly typed message "Call me. 555-9436."

Not recognizing the number, she picked up the phone and punched in the digits. She listened to three rings, then heard the click of an answering machine engaging.

"This is Case. Leave a message at the tone."

She clutched the receiver to her ear, too stunned to move. The tone sounded and she fumbled the phone, in her haste to disconnect the call.

Case sent her flowers? she thought in dismay. And yellow roses, no less, her absolute favorite. How had he known? And the silver toad vase…it was adorable, perfect. She collected toads in every shape and form.

But why would Case send her flowers?

"Doesn't matter," she told herself sternly. Whatever his reason, she wasn't interested. Not in him. Not in the roses. Not in the adorable silver toad he'd chosen to send them in. She was tossing it all out. She wasn't keeping a gift from Case Fortune.

She stooped to gather the arrangement into her arms and moaned pitifully when she found herself looking into the jeweled eyes of the silver toad. How could she throw away a toad? It would be like tossing out a friend.

Straightening, she snatched up the card and tore it into little pieces. She might keep the arrangement, but she wasn't calling him. She didn't care how much she liked yellow roses or how adorable she thought the silver toad vase, she was *not* calling Case Fortune. Not even to say thanks. Emily Post might have a heart attack over the slight, but etiquette be damned. Gina wasn't calling Case, nor was she sending a polite note of thanks.

She wanted nothing to do with Case Fortune.

Ever.

"Your personal taxi is here!"

Busy packing her briefcase for her trip to New York, Gina glanced up to find Zoie, her neighbor from across the hall, entering her loft. Zoie was the only person Gina had entrusted with a key to her loft, an honor Zoie took full advantage of by coming and going as she pleased.

Today Zoie had her hair spiked with purple mousse and, if Gina wasn't mistaken, was sporting a new tattoo on the back of her hand.

Shaking her head at her neighbor's bizarre taste, Gina set her briefcase on the floor. "All ready. I just need to grab my rolling bag."

Zoie stopped short, her eyes going wide, as she got her first glimpse of the flowers that filled the room. "Girl, have you given up writing and opened a floral shop?"

Grimacing, Gina shrugged on her coat. "No, but it looks like it, doesn't it?"

Zoie flicked a nail over a petal in a bouquet of forget-me-nots, then turned to Gina, her lips pursed in annoyance. "Obviously you've been holding out on me. Who's the guy?"

Gina shuddered at the mere thought of a relationship with Case. "Trust me, there is no guy."

Zoie spread her arms, indicating the flowers that filled every available space. "Then why all this?"

Gina heaved a sigh. "I wish I knew. It started with the yellow roses over there," she said pointing. "They were delivered on Monday. Tuesday morning I received the bucket of daisies. Later that day, the orchids arrived. Wednesday, the gladiolas and the basket of peonies. Yesterday the forget-me-nots and that tall palm plant in the corner."

"Nothing today?"

She tipped her head toward the screen that partitioned her bedroom from the remainder of the loft. "In there. I ran out of room in here."

"The guy must be crazy in love with you. Get a load of these orchids, will you? This time of year these things cost a small fortune."

Gina grimaced at the word *fortune*. "Trust me. He can afford it. And he's *not* in love with me. Heck, he doesn't even know me!"

"Mm-hmm," Zoie hummed doubtfully.

"It's true, I swear. We met for the first time last Saturday at my booksigning."

Zoie clasped her hands together in a dramatic plea of supplication. "Please tell me he's legal and not one of your adoring under-aged fans."

"Yes, Miss Drama Queen, he's legal."

"Does he have a name?"

"Case Fortune."

Zoie's eyes shot wide. "*The* Case Fortune?"

Irritated by her friend's reaction, Gina scowled. "You make him sound like some kind of God or something."

"According to the society page, he is."

"Trust me, he's not."

Zoie narrowed an eye. "I thought you said you didn't know him."

"I don't. But I know enough men like him to know what he's like."

"And that would be…" Zoie prompted.

"Heartless, selfish, driven." She lifted a brow. "Need I go on?"

"Unless I'm mistaken, those are the same personality traits I've heard you attribute to your father."

"Two peas in a pod."

"Come on, Gina," Zoie groused. "Give the guy a break. Just because your father's a jerk, doesn't mean all men are."

Gina jutted her chin. "I never said they were." She stooped and picked up her briefcase, signaling an end to the discussion. "We'd better go. With airport security being what it is, I don't want to take a chance on being late and missing my flight."

Zoie grasped the handle of Gina's rolling bag and

pulled it behind her as she followed Gina to the door. "You haven't forgotten that I'm going to Sully's for a couple of days and won't be here to pick you up when you return?"

"I haven't forgotten."

"So how are you going to get home?"

"I'll grab a cab."

Zoie bit back a smile as she stepped out into the hall. "You know, you could ask Case to pick you up. I'm sure he wouldn't mind."

Gina huffed a breath. "I'd walk first."

Two

Gina's drive home from the airport following her trip to New York was slow, due to the snow that had begun to fall a few hours earlier. But she didn't mind the delay. It wasn't as if she had anyone waiting for her at home. Not even Zoie. Besides, she loved snow.

Pressing her face against the side window, she watched the flakes drift down from a dark, leaden sky. As a young girl, she remembered standing outside with her face tipped up and her mouth open, trying to catch snowflakes as they fell. Her mother had always teased her, saying she looked like a baby bird begging to be fed.

She smiled sadly at the memory. She missed her mother. Missed the late night talks they used to have, the mornings spent curled up on the sofa in the sunroom, her head in her mother's lap. She closed her eyes, remembering the feel of her mother's fingers combing through her hair, the sound of her soft laughter as Gina entertained her with the stories she'd made up as a young girl.

You should write these stories down before you forget them. You might want to publish them someday.

"I did, Mama," she whispered to her reflection on the glass.

"What was that, ma'am?"

She turned from the window to find the taxi driver looking at her in the rearview mirror. Embarrassed, she averted her gaze. "Sorry. Just thinking out loud."

"Almost there," he announced. "And none too soon. They're saying we might get a foot or more before morning."

She glanced out the window again and smiled. "The kids will love it. Snowball fights. Building snowmen. They'll have a blast."

He looked at her in the rearview mirror. "You got kids?"

"Me?" she asked in surprise, then sputtered a laugh. "No. I'm not married."

He gave his head a woeful shake. "Don't need a marriage license to have kids. Not nowadays. Folks have gone plumb crazy, thinking a single person can raise a child alone. Takes two, I say," he said, with a decisive jerk of his chin. "A mother *and* a father."

Gina turned her face to the window again, thinking of her own family. The absentee father and the desperate-to-please mother.

Sometimes even two aren't enough, she thought sadly.

"Here we are," he said. "Want me to let you off out front or would you rather I take you to the parking garage?"

"Front is fine."

While the driver collected her suitcase from the trunk, Gina counted out the fare from her wallet, then slipped the straps of her purse and briefcase over her shoulder and climbed out. A snowflake landed on the end of her nose, making her laugh.

"Thanks for the ride," she said, as she handed the driver the fare. "You be careful out tonight."

He tipped his hat. "Same to you, ma'am."

Taking the handle of her rolling bag, Gina turned for her building, pulling the bag behind her. Lights glowed from behind the double front doors' leaded glass windows and spilled over onto the snow that had collected on the front steps.

"Welcome home."

She stumbled a step at the greeting, losing her grip on the handle of her rolling bag, and whirled to find a man stepping from the shadows at the corner of her building. With his hands in his pockets, his shoulders hunched against the cold and a watch cap pulled low over his brow, he looked like a mugger. Although muggings were rare in her neighborhood, they weren't unheard of. Fearing she was about to become the next victim, she glanced down the street, praying the taxi driver was still within hearing range. But the vehicle was already two blocks away, too far for the driver to hear if she were to scream.

"How was your trip?"

Recognizing the voice of her would-be attacker, she whipped her head back around.

"Case?" she said in disbelief. Sagging weakly, she pressed a hand against her heart to still its panicked beating. "Good grief. You scared a year off my life."

He dragged the cap from his head. "Sorry. That wasn't my intent."

Feeling foolish for mistaking him for a mugger, she hitched her purse higher on her shoulder. "What are you doing here anyway?"

"I came to welcome you home from your trip."

She eyed him suspiciously. "How did you know I was out of town?"

"One of your neighbors told me. Zoie, I believe was her name. When the florist called to tell me they were unable to deliver the flowers I sent, I became concerned. Thought I'd better check and make sure you were all right. Zoie was leaving as I arrived and she told me you'd gone to New York on a business trip."

Gina made a mental note to tell Zoie to mind her own business in the future. "As you can see, I'm fine."

He gave her a slow look up and down, a lazy smile chipping at one corner of his mouth. "Better than fine, I'd say."

She stiffened her spine, refusing to fall for a line as obvious as that. "If you'll excuse me, it's been an exhausting day." She stooped to retrieve her rolling bag, but Case was quicker.

He righted the bag, then bowed slightly, opening a hand in invitation. "Lead the way."

She squared her shoulders and stood her ground. "I'm more than capable of carrying my own bag."

"I'm sure you are," he said amiably. "But my mother would roll over in her grave if she knew I'd stood by and allowed a woman to carry her own bags."

She hesitated, not wanting his assistance, then huffed a breath and marched for the front door, leaving him to follow. After quickly dealing with the security code, she thrust out her hand for her bag.

He angled his body to block her and nodded toward the door. "Ladies first."

Setting her jaw, she strode inside and straight for the elevator. "This really isn't necessary," she said irritably.

"Indulge me."

She shot him a frown, as the elevator door opened, then rolled her eyes and stepped inside.

He followed, maneuvering the bag onto the elevator.

"You didn't call me."

She spared him a glance, then turned her face to the display, watching as the numbers lit, indicating their ascent. "No, I didn't."

The elevator doors opened onto her floor, the door to her loft directly opposite. She stepped out and Case followed, pulling her bag behind him.

She dealt with the lock, then turned to face him. "Thank you for your assistance. I can handle things from here."

He nodded. "I'd like to see you again."

"Why?" she asked bluntly.

He shrugged. "Why not?"

"I've already told you that I don't care for men like you."

"How can you know what kind of man I am, when you don't even know me?"

"I know enough to know I'm not interested."

When she turned away, he caught her arm and drew her back around. Set against his dark navy pea coat, his eyes seemed incredibly blue...and determined.

"Give me a chance," he said. "Go out with me.

Forget whatever it is you've heard about me and judge for yourself what kind of man I am."

She gulped, wanting to refuse him, to avoid the disappointments she knew she would be setting herself up for. She knew what kind of man he was. He was just like her father.

But how could she say no to a man who adhered to his mother's teachings, even when his mother wasn't around to fuss at him when he didn't? A man so unbelievably handsome, it made her teeth ache just to look at him? Besides, it wasn't as if she received invitations for dates all that often. By design or destiny—she was never sure which—she had few friends, male or female.

"All right," she said grudgingly. "I'll go out with you, but just this—"

Before she could finish, his mouth was on hers. Caught off-guard, she had to brace a hand against his chest to keep from stumbling backwards.

She should have been insulted that he'd take such advantage of her, demand that he release her. This was exactly the kind of behavior she'd expected from him, a selfish disregard for a woman's needs or feelings.

Yet, there was a confidence in his kiss, a seductiveness that kept her silent, made her want to experience more.

The chill of outdoors clung to his coat. She felt it beneath her palm, as well as the moisture from the snow that had seeped into the wool fabric. Deeper still she lost herself in the rhythmic beat of his heart, the heat from his body.

By the time he withdrew, her knees were weak, her mind fuzzy, her breath locked somewhere inside her chest.

He crooked a finger beneath her chin, his smile leaning toward the cocky side of confident. "I'll pick you up tomorrow at noon. Dress warm."

She gulped, unable to tear her gaze from his. "Okay," she murmured dully, then turned into her loft, her lips still tingling from the pressure of his.

By noon the following day, Gina had all but convinced herself that Case's kiss wasn't all she'd built it up in her mind to be. He'd caught her completely off-guard, which alone would make the kiss probably seem more than what it really was. She had to consider, too, that men like Case were excellent actors. If a situation called for knocking a woman off her feet with a mind-blowing kiss, she had no doubt he could deliver one…and feel absolutely no remorse afterwards for the deception.

In spite of changing her opinion about his kiss, she'd decided to stick to her agreement to go out with him. Attempting to wiggle her way out of the commitment seemed more trouble than it was worth, considering the man's stubbornness. It exhausted her to even think of trying.

Which was why she was currently sitting beside him on the Trolley, dressed in her warmest clothes, as he'd suggested. She'd been surprised when he'd guided her to the Trolley stop at the corner of her block, rather than to the vehicle parked at the curb in front of her building. She'd assumed a man of Case's position would consider public transportation beneath him. Especially when his Cadillac Escalade was parked right in front of her building and he was more than capable of driving them himself.

She stole a glance at him beneath her lashes, wondering if this might be an indication she'd misjudged him.

As if sensing her gaze, he looked her way and smiled. "Warm enough?"

She forced a polite smile in return. "I'm fine." Unable to think of anything else to say, she turned her face to the window as the Trolley stopped to pick up more passengers. "Where are we going?" she asked curiously.

"The Falls."

She snapped her head around to stare at him. "The *Falls*?"

"Yeah. Hope you don't mind. They're beautiful in the summertime, but I like them best in the winter when there's snow on the ground and the river is starting to freeze."

"The Falls," she repeated, having a hard time imagining *the* Case Fortune finding pleasure in visiting what most would consider a tourist attraction.

"You don't mind, do you? We can go somewhere else if you'd prefer."

She shook her head. "No, I love the Falls. I'm just surprised that you'd want to go there."

Smiling, he caught her hand and brought it to hold against his thigh. "I make it a point to visit them at least once a month. More, when I can find the time."

Aware of the hand that held hers and the casualness with which he'd made the connection, she swallowed hard, praying her palm wouldn't perspire and give away her nervousness.

He angled his head to look at her. "Have you ever seen the view from the Observation Tower?"

"Y-yes, but it's been years."

"Then we'll definitely include that in our plans. I thought we'd stop off at the Horse Barn, too. There's an art exhibit today."

Gina knew all about the Horse Barn Arts Center and the current exhibit on display. She was a member of the Arts Council and attended every exhibit the Council sponsored. In fact, she had planned on seeing the current exhibit next weekend. It was a hands-on display designed for the entertainment and education of children. Though it was right up her alley, she had a hard time envisioning Case enjoying anything even remotely juvenile.

"What would you like to do first?" he asked. "The Tower or the Horse Barn?"

She considered a moment. "The Tower. That way we can warm up afterwards at the Horse Barn."

Within minutes they arrived at the Trolley's last stop, the Visitor's Center. From there they walked to the Falls. The snow from the night before had fallen short of the weatherman's forecast of twelve inches, leaving only three or four inches to cover the ground. In spite of the snow and the cold, Gina found the walk invigorating.

Even before the falls came into view, she heard the sound of the water crashing over the rocks. Snow lay in drifts along the banks of the river and blanketed the trees in soft, white canopies, while icicles hung in glittering spikes from the massive rocks that formed the falls.

"Come on," Case caught her hand. "Let's get a little closer."

Gina allowed him to tug her along behind him. When he stopped, he wrapped an arm around her waist and drew her against his side.

As they stood, taking in the sight and sounds, a memory surfaced, one which mimicked almost perfectly her current position. She'd been maybe ten at the time, standing beside the falls with her mother, watching the water rush over the rocks. Her mother had said something that day that Gina hadn't thought much of at the time.

I wonder if drowning is painful?

At the time, Gina hadn't thought too much of her mother's comment—other than it was a macabre thing to say. Hearing it had sent chills chasing down her spine. But it wasn't until after her mother's suicide that she'd realized that her mother had been considering taking her own life for quite a while before actually committing the act.

Shivering at the memory, she forced it from her mind.

Case looked down at her. "Cold?" he asked, raising his voice to make himself heard over the sound of the falls.

Rather than tell him the reason for the shiver, she decided to accept the excuse he offered. "A little."

He unbuttoned his overcoat and drew her back against his chest, wrapping his coat around her and holding it in place by hugging his arms around her middle. "Better?" he asked.

Painfully aware of the body pressed against hers, she could only nod.

He turned his face against her ear to make himself heard over the Falls. "Do you remember what a mess this area used to be? Lots of work went into cleaning it up and making it the attraction it is today."

Frowning, she angled her head to peer up at him. "You sound as if you had a hand in the project."

"Not as much as I would've liked. Dakota Fortunes helped fund the clean-up, supplying equipment, as well as man-power to do the work. I worked when I could, but it took the efforts of hundreds of men to complete the job."

Surprised to learn that he had willingly volunteered his time for a public project, she filed away that new insight into his character to consider later.

"Reynolds Refining contributed, too," he went on. "Money, as well as fuel. But I'm sure you knew about that."

She shook her head. "No. I know very little about my father's company."

She half expected him to quiz her more about her relationship with her father and his business and was relieved when he let the subject drop and resumed talking about the restoration of the falls.

Gina had thoroughly enjoyed spending the day with Case. But now that it was coming to an end, her inexperience with men and dating in general left her in a quandary about the proper end-of-date protocol. Invite him in? Kiss? No kiss?

Unsure, she unlocked the door to her loft, then

turned, deciding it safest to simply follow his lead. "Thanks for the day. I really had a good time."

Teasing her with a smile, he caught her elbows and drew her to him. "Does this mean you've changed your opinion of me?"

She lowered her gaze, embarrassed that she'd said such awful things to his face. "Let's just say I have new data to consider."

Chuckling, he bussed her a quick kiss. "I guess I'll have to accept that for now."

"I guess you will."

"When can I see you again?"

"Well, I don't know," she stammered, surprised that he appeared to want to take her out again. "While I was in New York, the art director requested changes on some of the illustrations for my next book and wants them ASAP."

"How long are we talking? Days? Weeks? Months?"

She couldn't help but laugh at his frustrated tone. "I don't know. It depends on my creative muse. A couple of days probably."

"I could help," he offered.

She gave him a doubtful look. "I think you're forgetting I saw some of your drawings at the Art Center."

"I may not be an artist, but I'd make a damn good model." He waggled his brows. "Nudes are my specialty."

She blushed furiously, easily able to imagine him naked. "I—I don't do nudes."

"Spoil sport," he grumbled, then sighed. "Call me when you're done and we'll celebrate." He looked down his nose at her. "You *do* have my number."

She flushed guiltily at the reminder that she'd ignored his requests on all the cards accompanying the flowers he'd sent her. "Yes, I have it."

He kissed her again, this one longer than the one before, then gave her a push toward her open door. "Get to work. The longer you goof off, the longer it'll be before I can see you again."

Dazed, she lifted a hand in farewell, then closed the door and leaned back against it, listening to the elevator doors swish close behind Case and the muffled grind of cable as the elevator started its descent.

He'd kissed her. Really kissed her. And he wanted to see her again.

With a dreamy sigh, she pushed away from the door and started toward her work table. She hadn't taken three steps in that direction, when she heard the scrape of a key in her lock and the sound of the door opening. She glanced back just as Zoie came charging in.

"Spill, girl," Zoie ordered, "and don't leave anything out."

Though she knew Zoie was referring to Case, Gina gave her a blank look. "About what?"

Zoie tossed up her hands. "About *him!* Case Fortune. I saw his Escalade parked out front when I got home from Sully's. Sully sends his love, by the way," she added.

"Sully's such a sweetie," she said fondly, then narrowed an eye at Zoie. "And how you do you know that was Case's Escalade? Did you pick the lock and go through his glove compartment?"

"Didn't have to. He has one of those Dakota Fortune parking passes hanging from his rearview mirror. Kinda hard to miss."

"Oh."

"No apology? Just, oh?" Chuckling, she flapped a hand. "Forget it. Now tell me where you've been all day. I've been climbing the walls, waiting for you to get home."

Gina turned back to her desk and picked up her portfolio. "Here and there," she replied vaguely.

"Uh-uh," Zoie warned, trailing after her. "That's not good enough." She flopped down on the sofa and folded her arms across her chest. "I want to know every gory detail, starting with how you hooked up, all the way to the kiss I saw him plant on you in the hallway, and I'm not leaving until you tell all."

Knowing her friend would make good her threat,

Gina crossed to the sofa and sat down. "He was waiting for me when I got home last night." She shot Zoie a frown. "Thanks to a nosy neighbor who can't keep her mouth shut."

Unfazed, Zoie tucked her feet beneath her, her expression expectant. "So? Did he spend the night?"

"Heavens, no!" Gina cried, shocked by the suggestion. "He carried my luggage to the door and asked me out. Period."

Zoie's face fell in disappointment. "Bummer. So what did you do today?"

"We went to Falls Park, took in the exhibit at the Horse Barn Art Center, and had dinner at that new Italian restaurant on Phillips Street."

"Ah, come on," Zoie groused. "That's tour guide stuff. I want the juice. Physical contact. Whispered words of endearment. That kind of thing."

"He held my hand. Does that count?"

"Stiff or foreplay?"

Gina looked at her askance. "What the heck does that mean?"

"Stiff is like dead fingers. No movement. Foreplay is playful, sensual. Thumb strokes on the palm. Little squeezes of the fingers. Which was it?"

Gina frowned a moment thinking. "Foreplay," she decided.

Zoie rubbed her hands together in glee. "Oh, man. That's good. Real good. What else?"

"While we were walking, he put his arm around my shoulders a couple of times. And he snuggled me up inside his coat when we were standing by the Falls."

"Back to front or front to front?"

"Back to front."

"Did you feel anything? Like a hard-on, I mean."

"Zoie!" Gina cried.

Zoie held up her hands. "Okay, okay. Just trying to get a bead on his level of attraction."

"It was one date," Gina reminded her drolly. "It's a little early to start thinking about sex."

Zoie opened her hands. "Hey. Sex knows no time-line. When the time's right, it's right. You've got to learn to open up a little bit. Go with the flow."

Gina winced. "I don't know how."

"Relax, you mean?"

Gina nodded.

"Alcohol," Zoie said without hesitation. "Nothing loosens up a person's inhibitions quicker than a stiff drink or two."

Shaking her head, Gina pushed to her feet. "I'm not much of a drinker."

"Good. That means it would take less to get you going."

Sputtering a laugh, Gina planted her hands on her hips. "You are a real case, you know it? Here you are telling me to get drunk and have sex with a man I hardly know."

"Do you want to remain a virgin the rest of your life?"

Gina winced, then shook her head. "No."

"Does Case ring your bell?"

Gina rolled her eyes. "If you're asking if I'm attracted to him, yes."

Zoie shrugged. "Well, there you have it. Case Fortune is your frog-prince, the guy who's going to introduce you to the wild side of life, teach you the old bump and grind."

Gina clapped her hands over her cheeks, her face flaming. "I can't believe we're even having this discussion."

Zoie unfolded her legs and rose. Slinging an arm around Gina's shoulders, she drew her with her as she walked to the door. "Sister, it's time. Past time, if you ask me. You've been wearing that chastity belt long enough."

Three

At the moment, Gina felt more like a voodoo priestess than she did an author of children's books.

Candles surrounded her work table, filling the loft with flickering light and the calming scent of lavender. Sounds of the ocean, specifically chosen for its soothing qualities, played from her stereo speakers. A bowl of cheese—flavored crackers mixed with chocolate candies—both known for having produced restorative powers in the past— was in easy reach of her hand. Her good luck toad sat on his perch on the crooked arm of her task light, overseeing her work. She'd even changed into her oldest and most ragged sweat suit. The one with the hole in the left sleeve and the streak of hot pink fingernail polish on the thigh. The same one she'd been wearing when she'd received the call from the publishing company, telling her they wanted to buy her first book.

She'd tried every trick in the book to jump-start her creative muse, but so far not a one of them had worked.

And it was all Case's fault.

Or, rather, Zoie's, she corrected with a frown.

Zoie was the one who had put the idea of sleeping with Case in her mind. And now that was all she could think about. Besides the would-he, could-she, should-she worries that would plague any virgin considering making the fall, she kept imagining what kind of lover Case would be.

And when she wasn't worrying about the act itself, she was stressing over the man she was considering giving herself to.

Prior to Sunday and her outing with Case, she hadn't known him personally, and what she had known, she hadn't particularly liked. As far as she was concerned, he was cut from the same pin-stripe-cloth as her father, which was reason enough to dislike him—or, at the very least, distrust him. Businessmen like Case and her father were incapable of maintaining personal relationships. Not the kind of relationship Gina wanted and needed from a man. Men like them devoted all their time, energy and emotions to the companies they ran. Company first, family somewhere way down the line. That was the motto they lived by.

Hadn't Gina witnessed enough of her own mother's frustrations and disappointments married to a man obsessed with his business to know she wanted no part of that life? Hadn't she purposely chosen a career on the opposite end of the spectrum from her father's for that same reason? Hadn't she shut her father out of her life because he'd always chosen business over family? It hadn't been a decision she'd made rashly or without proper justification.

It had been a means of survival.

As a young girl, troubled by the tension and unhappiness in her home, she'd created a fairy tale world to retreat to, a safe and happy place filled with the characters she created in her mind. After her mother's suicide, when her father had packed her up and shipped her off to boarding school, she'd taken those fairy tale characters with her, relying on them for the emotional support and comfort her father was incapable of supplying. As an adult, she'd taken those same characters and the stories she'd made up about them and spun them into a cash cow that currently paid the bills, which had given her the ability to sever her financial dependence on her father and, in a sense, thumb her nose at him and his way of life.

And now she was considering sleeping with a man from her father's world? The world she hated, despised, shunned?

She dropped her elbows to her desk and her head to her hands. "Oh, God," she moaned miserably. "What was I thinking?"

She needed to forget Case Fortune and focus her mind on toads. Timothy Toad, specifically. Timothy Toad was her friend, her redeemer. He was the only male she could count on, the only one who had never let her down. He had no faults, no ulterior motives, no hidden agendas. He was perfect in every way.

There was only one problem. Two, actually, if she considered the fact that Timothy Toad was a figment of her imagination.

Timothy might be a male, but he wasn't a *man*.

Yawning, Gina rubbed her fists against her eyes, trying to scrub away the webs of weariness. It was pushing midnight on day eight of her deadline and she wanted nothing more than to go to bed. But sleep was out of the question until she'd made the requested changes on the illustrations.

Glum, she poked a toe at the wads of paper littering the floor around her feet. Each represented a failed attempt at giving the art director what he wanted. She'd been at it for a week and she was no closer to capturing on paper the art director's concept than she had been when she had started.

Firming her jaw, she snatched up the pencil again and held it over the blank piece of paper.

"It's because you're not concentrating hard enough," she lectured sternly. "You know the story. Heck, you wrote it! Just draw the images and emotions that are in your head."

Hoping to jumpstart her creative juices, she pressed the lead to the paper, drew a circle, then leaned back and studied it, waiting for the image hiding inside to reveal itself. Something flashed by the window, catching her eye, and she glanced up in alarm.

But the only thing she saw was her own image reflected in the dark glass.

"Now you're seeing things," she muttered under her breath. "Next thing you know you'll be talking to yourself."

She clapped a hand over her mouth, realizing it was too late. She already was.

Something struck the glass and she snapped her head up in time to see a flash of white, before it dropped beneath the ledge and disappeared from sight. Her heart thudding wildly, she stood and leaned to peer out. Frustrated by the drafting table that stood between her and the window, she shifted around to its end and pushed it out of her way.

Another flash of white streaked past her peripheral vision and she whirled to the window to look out, watching as the white object drifted slowly down. Paper? she asked herself. Whatever it was it couldn't be anything more substantial than paper or it would have made a more of a sound when it hit the window.

She shifted her gaze to the sidewalk directly below her window and saw a man standing beneath the street light. A vandal, she thought, her anger surging. Prepared to give the guy a piece of her mind, she shoved up the window. "What do you think you're doing down there?" she shouted furiously. "If you don't leave this instant, I'm calling the police."

The man tipped his head back and looked up.

She gaped. "Case?"

"Stay right there!" he shouted, then darted over to pick up the paper from the ground.

"What are you doing?" she cried.

"Sending you an airmail message." He reared his arm back and sent the white object flying.

When she saw that the paper airplane was going to come short of making it to her window, she leaned out and grabbed it, managing to catch it by the tip of a wing. Ducking back inside, she read the message scrawled inside.

It's been a week. No calls. Toad lovers need hugs, too.

She pressed her fingers against her lips, her heart melting at the last line, then let out a laugh and leaned out the window and called down to him, "You're crazy."

"No I'm not. I'm lonely. Can I come up? It's freezing out here."

She winced, remembering her earlier decision to forget Case Fortune. "It's kind of late," she hedged.

"It's not like you're asleep or anything," he pointed out. "Come on, Gina. At least give me a chance to warm up."

She vacillated a moment longer, then caved, telling herself it was cold outside and he probably *was* freezing. "Okay. But just for a minute."

She closed the window, then stooped to scoop up the wadded balls of paper and stuff them into the waste basket. She didn't want him to see the evidence of her creative block.

She heard the muffled sound of the elevator making its ascent and hurried to the door, combing her fingers through her straggly hair.

When she opened the door, Case was stepping off the elevator. He was dressed casually for a change. Boots, jeans, a black sweater beneath a leather jacket. His hair was mussed—probably from the watch cap he'd dragged off his head and shoved into a pocket of his jacket—and his cheeks were ruddy from the cold. If possible, he looked even more handsome than he did when wearing a business suit.

She groaned inwardly, remembering her ragged sweats and the lime green fuzzy socks that covered her feet.

A slow smile spread across his face. "Hi, gorgeous."

She ducked her head and wound a strand of hair behind her ear. "I look a mess."

"You look wonderful to me."

Before she could call him the liar he was, he put his hands on her shoulders and backed her into her loft.

"Seven days, three hours and thirty-two minutes," he said, as he kicked the door closed behind him.

She blinked at him in confusion. "What?"

"That's how long I've been wanting to do this."

Before she realized his intent, he covered her mouth with his. She didn't want to kiss him, she told herself. And she didn't want *him* kissing *her.*

Or did she?

She might have mentally decided she never wanted to see him again, but her body didn't appear to have received the message. Without conscious thought, she was leaning into him, her breasts pressed against the muscled wall of his chest, her face tipped up to his. His hands slid to her back, his palms urging her closer still, and she responded, lifting her arms and looping them around his neck.

Strong. Possessive. Demanding. His kiss mirrored exactly the character traits she'd attributed to him, yet she didn't find his kiss in the least bit repulsive. In fact, she found it intoxicating, invigorating, exciting.

He framed her face between his hands and drew back with a satisfied sigh to press his lips against her forehead.

"I've been thinking about doing that all week."

His voice sounded rusty, the admission dragged from a place deep inside him. She'd been thinking about kissing him, too, but couldn't have uttered a word if her life had depended on it.

He tipped her face higher, his expression filled with reproach.

"Why haven't you called?"

"I—I haven't finished the drawings."

He glanced toward her drawing table, where the task light cast a circle of light over her sketch pad. "You were working?"

She nodded.

"And I interrupted you," he said with regret.

She shrugged. "No biggie. I wasn't making much progress anyway."

He shifted his gaze back to hers, a smile teasing

one corner of his mouth. "Would thinking about me having anything to do with that?"

She stared, at first horrified that he somehow knew the cause of her creative block, then pursed her lips. "Your ego is showing."

He slipped his hands beneath the hem of her sweatshirt and drew her hips to his. "I was thinking about you. Couldn't get a thing done all week."

She gulped, remembering Zoie quizzing her about the hard-on and trying not to think about that. "Y-you're just saying that."

He dipped his head and nuzzled his nose behind her ear. "Now, why would I lie to you?"

An hour ago—heck, five minutes ago!—she could've named a hundred reasons why he would. But at the moment she couldn't think of anything beyond his mouth, his taste, and how much she wished he would kiss her again.

"Case—"

Even as she spoke his name, he slid his mouth to hers, his hands in a slow journey up her ribs. Heat flamed in her middle and fanned to every extremity, stealing her breath, as his thumbs nudged the undersides of her breasts.

She heard a moan and inwardly cringed when she realized the sound had come from her. She'd die before she'd let him know how inexperienced she was—or how needy. But he didn't appear to have heard her. He was much too busy teasing her tongue with his and stroking her breasts.

This is it, she thought wildly, as electrical shocks ricocheted through her body. This is what desire feels like. She'd thought she'd experienced it before, but she'd been *so* wrong. *This* was raw, mind-consuming, nerve-burning lust, the kind that made a woman say to hell with discretion and propriety, rip off her clothes and throw herself at a man.

Realizing how close she was to losing control, she tried to get a grip on her emotions. She wouldn't give herself to Case. Couldn't. She knew how much pain men like him were capable of inflicting.

Knowing this, she pressed her hands against his chest. "Case. No."

"Come on, baby," he murmured, rubbing his groin seductively against hers. "You want this. We both do."

She clamped her fingers around his forearms and dragged his hands from beneath her sweatshirt. "Whether I do or not isn't the point. I'm saving myself for the man I marry."

His face went slack. "You're a virgin?"

Embarrassment burned her cheeks, but she nodded.

He dragged a hand over his hair. "Well, that certainly puts a different spin on things."

She looked at him in puzzlement. "What's that supposed to mean?"

He shook his head. "Nothing."

"Look," she said, her frustration returning. "If you're only here for sex, you might as well leave. I've got work to do."

He hesitated a moment, then shrugged off his jacket. "No. I'm staying."

Stunned, she watched him cross to her desk and pluck the illustration she'd been working on from the wallboard where she'd tacked it.

He glanced over his shoulder at her. "Is this one of the drawings the art director asked you to change?"

She wrinkled her nose at the reminder. "One of four."

He sank down on her stool, studying the drawing. "The guy must be blind. This is really good."

Shaking her head, she moved to stand beside him. "No. He was right. The expression is all wrong." She pointed at Timothy Toad's face. "He's supposed to be sad, and he looks… I don't know. Bored."

"What's wrong with bored?"

"Nothing, except in the story, he's just lost his best friend. He should be…sad."

Case picked up a pencil, offered it to her. "Show me."

She tucked her hand behind her back. Her art was a private thing, something she did alone, never in front of an audience. "I really don't like for people to watch me work."

He shifted her to stand between his knees. "I promise, I won't look."

Mindful of his stubbornness, she snatched the pencil from his hand. Hoping to get rid of him, she quickly drew a rough sketch of Timothy's face, turning the corners of his mouth down. She paused a moment to study the drawing and her eyes sharpened, as she saw, not only the difference in the emotion from the original sketch, but the direction she needed to continue. She quickly drew in a fat tear drop leaking from his eye, then added a reflection of Timothy's friend's face shimmering in the moisture.

"That's it!" she cried, turning to throw her arms around Case's neck and hug him tight. "That's exactly the emotion I've been searching for."

Oblivious now to Case's presence, the fact that she had an audience, *or* that she had wanted him to leave, she spun back around, flipped the page and began to sketch in earnest, the pencil all but flying over the page.

Gina opened her eyes to bright sunlight gleaming through the floor to ceiling windows of her bedroom and stretched lazily. Waking to sunshine was an oddity for her, as her bedroom faced west, not east.

But when a person slept the day away, she reminded herself, she couldn't expect the sun to follow suit.

Fueled by a creative burst of energy, she'd worked through the night, completing all four of the illustrations requiring changes by her art director. She'd finished the last just before sunrise and had crawled fully dressed into bed. Case had left shortly thereafter. She wasn't sure of the exact time of his departure, as she'd been too exhausted to look at the clock. But she remembered him pulling the covers over her and tucking her in. She also remembered feeling the light scrape of his beard, as he'd placed a kiss on her cheek and hearing the huskiness of his whispered "goodnight."

She drew the covers to her nose to hide her smile. She couldn't believe he'd stayed all night. He'd remained right with her throughout her creative frenzy, never once complaining or appearing as if he was bored or anxious to leave. She'd stood between his knees while working on the first two illustrations, with him watching over her shoulder. And when she'd grown weary of standing, he'd pulled her onto his lap and looped an arm around her waist, holding her there while she completed the last two.

What kind of man would do something like that? she asked herself. Certainly not the kind of man she'd accused Case of being. There had been nothing selfish or self-serving in his behavior. And his comments had been encouraging and supportive, not negative or demeaning. In fact, without him, she doubted she would've been able to make the needed changes. His probing questions were what had finally unleashed her creative block and helped her find the images and emotions she'd needed to complete the task. And it was his supportive presence that had given her the ability to stick with the task throughout the long night until she'd finished the last one.

The telephone rang and she glanced at the extension on her bedside table, somehow knowing it was Case. After the second ring, she picked up the receiver.

"Hello?"

"Good morning."

A shiver chased down her spine at the sound of his voice and she sank back against her pillow, hugging the receiver to her ear. "It's afternoon," she reminded him.

"Did I wake you?"

"No. I was awake."

"Did you sleep well?"

"Like the dead. How about you?"

"The same. I had no idea drawing was so exhausting."

She hid a smile. "I don't remember you holding a pencil."

"Didn't I?" His chuckle rumbled across the airwaves to her ear. "Then explain why my fingers are cramped?"

"That was probably from holding me on your lap all night."

A lusty sigh crossed the airwaves. "Yeah. That must've been it." There was a stretch of silence, then he asked, "Do you have plans for dinner?"

She blinked in surprise at the sudden change in topic. "Well, no. I haven't even thought about food."

"Then have dinner with me. My parents just returned from Australia and all the family is gathering at the estate to welcome them home."

She clutched the phone tighter to her ear, panic tightening her chest at the thought of meeting his family. "I wouldn't want to intrude on a family celebration."

"You wouldn't be intruding. It's nothing fancy. Just a chance to welcome them home. Besides, they'll love having you join us."

"I don't know, Case," she said doubtfully. "I'm an only child. I don't have much experience with big families."

"Tell you what," he offered. "Dinner isn't scheduled until seven. I'll pick you up at six. Give you the grand tour of the estate. That way you can meet some of the family prior to dinner and won't feel so overwhelmed."

Despite Case's assurance, Gina *was* overwhelmed. From the moment he'd turned onto the drive that wound its way through the Fortunes' one-hundred and seventy-five acre estate until he came to a stop in front of his family's home, she was struck dumb by the majesty of it all. Gothic in design, the mansion stood like a fortress against a gun-metal gray sky. Three stories of dark gray stone and scrolled ironwork made up the center portion of the house, with one-story wings jutting left and right. Gina counted a minimum of four chimneys rising from the black roof before she gave up and simply stared.

Case covered her hand with his. "Don't worry," he teased. "It may look haunted, but no ghosts live within those walls."

She released an uneasy breath. "That's good to know."

He climbed out and circled the hood to open her door.

"We'll save the outdoor tour for a warmer day," he told her, leading the way to the front door.

One step inside and Gina released the breath she'd been holding, as well as her fears of bumping into a ghost. While the outside of the mansion appeared cold and gloomy, the inside was filled with warmth and color.

Before she could take it all in, Case caught her hand and tugged her toward the split staircase, taking the set of stairs to the right. "First stop, my bedroom."

She jerked to a halt, pulling him to a standstill, as well. "You live here?" she asked in amazement.

"Along with my parents, brother Creed, half-brother Blake, and sister Eliza. Skylar, my half-sister, has a cottage on the estate, so I guess you'd say she lives here, too."

"Doesn't it get a little crowded? I mean, it's a huge house, but I'd think you'd want some privacy once in a while."

"When I do, I head for my penthouse on the top floor of the Dakota Fortunes' building. Creed has a penthouse there, too, but the units are totally separate. Even when we're there at the same time, we seldom see each other, unless we make a point to do so."

He gave her hand a tug. "Come on. There's lots to show you."

When they reached the second floor, he opened a door and bowed slightly. "My humble abode, madame."

Amused by his butler-like manner, she stepped inside and looked around, her eyes rounding, as her amusement gave way to shock. "Holy cow. You could drop my entire loft in here and have room left over."

He shrugged off his coat and draped it over a chair, then helped Gina remove hers. "It serves its purpose." He headed for the wet bar built into a corner of the room. "Would you like something to drink?"

"Just water for me, thanks."

While he poured their drinks, she looked around. Though beautifully decorated, it was obvious the suite belonged to a bachelor. A king-size platform bed dominated one wall. Draped neatly over it's top was a navy velvet duvet with a burned-out *F* monogrammed in its center. A sitting area held two overstuffed chairs upholstered in burgundy arranged for easy viewing of the plasma TV on the opposite wall. Framed paintings were arranged gallery-style to the left of the TV. Gina moved closer to study them.

"Here you go."

She accepted the glass Case offered her, then turned to peer at the portraits again. "Who is this?" she asked curiously, pointing to an oil of a woman dressed in a long evening gown and posed in a garden.

"My mother."

"She's beautiful."

"Yes, she was."

Puzzled by his use of past tense, she glanced at him in confusion. "Was?"

"She died when I was about six," he explained.

"But I thought you said your parents just returned from Australia?"

"My father and *step*-mother."

"Does that bother you?" she asked, unable to resist asking. "I mean, you obviously loved your

mother very much. I would think it would be difficult for you to accept your father remarrying and
bringing his new wife into the home he once shared
with your mother."

"Yes and no," he said. "Actually, my father has
married twice since my mother's death. I despised
my first step-mother and still do. Trina Watters is a
conniving witch, which my father finally realized
and divorced her. They had two children together,
Blake and Skylar. After he divorced Trina, he hired
Patricia, my current step-mother, as a nanny and
later married her."

He held up a hand. "I know what you're probably
thinking, and if you are, you're wrong. Patricia isn't
a gold-digger like Trina. In fact, it took Dad a long
time to convince Patricia to marry him."

Gina was blown-away by the twists and turns in
Case's family tree. "How on earth do you keep them
all straight?"

"Actually, there's one more. Maya Blackstone.
She's Patricia's daughter, which makes her my step-
sister." He nodded toward her drink. "Are you
finished? If you are, I want to show you the solarium."

After putting away their glasses, Case guided
her toward the door. "There's a pond and fountain
there," he told her, then shot her a wink. "I'll bet if
you look closely enough, you might even find a
toad or two hiding among the ferns."

Laughing, Gina walked with him down the stairs. As they reached the halfway point, Gina spotted a woman standing at the entry table in the hall below, thumbing through a stack of mail. The woman had a slender build and looked as if a strong wind could blow her over. As she watched, the woman suddenly froze, her eyes riveted on the envelope she held, then swayed slightly, as if she were about to faint.

Case must have noticed the woman's reaction, too, because he ran the rest of the way down the stairs and slid an arm around her to support her.

"Are you all right, Patricia?" he asked in concern.

She pressed a shaky hand to her forehead. "Just suffering a bit of jet lag, I guess." Forcing a reassuring smile, she patted his hand. "I'm fine now." She glanced at Gina and gave Case a chiding look. "Case Fortune," she scolded. "Where are your manners? Introduce me to your friend."

"Patricia, I'd like you to meet Gina Reynolds. Gina, my step-mother Patricia Blackstone Fortune."

Smiling shyly, Gina took the hand the woman offered. "It's a pleasure to meet you, Mrs. Fortune."

"Patricia," his step-mother insisted, then looked up at Case in question. "The two of you are staying for dinner, I hope?"

"Indeed we are," he assured her. "We're just making a quick trip to the solarium so that I can show Gina the pond and fountain."

"You might want to save that for after dinner," Patricia warned. "The others are already gathering in the dining room." She hugged the mail tighter against her chest. "I'll join you there, as soon as I put this away."

Case watched his step-mother walk away, his forehead creased in a frown.

"Is something wrong?" Gina asked in concern.

"Did she seem upset to you?"

"I don't know that I would term it 'upset,' but she definitely appeared shaken." She waved a dismissive hand. "It's probably nothing more than jet lag, just as she said."

"Maybe," he said doubtfully, then shrugged off his concern. "Well? Are you ready to meet the family?"

"Do I have a choice?"

Laughing, he looped her arm through his and guided her toward the dining room. "No. But don't worry. I'll stay right by your side all evening."

Four

Gina felt as if she had been dropped down in the middle of a nest of magpies…or, worse, the eye of a tornado. Her head ached, her ears rang, and though the food looked and smelled delicious, she hadn't managed so much as a bite. How could she, and hope to keep up with the conversations flying around her?

There are so many of them, was all she could think as she stole a glance down the length of the table at Case's family. Halves, wholes, steps. The one sibling of Case's she was confident she could address correctly was Creed, and that was only because he favored Case so much. In fact, the two could be mistaken for twins!

His parents were easily identified, as they were the oldest in the group. Nash, Case's father, could easily have been Case's brother, due to his youthful appearance and the features he shared with his sons. But the rest? Impossible! There were simply too many.

The sound of Case's voice forced her attention from her thoughts.

"Any mobsters tried to take over your casino yet, Blake?" Case asked the man across the table.

Everyone at the table howled with laughter—everyone, that is, except Blake. Gina watched his eyes narrow and his hands ball into fists, and thought for a moment he might leap across the table and grab Case by the throat.

"Are you questioning my ability to manage my own business?" he challenged tersely.

"Come on, Blake," Creed chided. "Where's your sense of humor? Case was only kidding."

"Yeah, Blake," Case agreed. "Can't you take a joke?"

A woman from the opposite end of the table spoke up. "I think he lost that ability when Dad turned Dakota Fortunes over to you and Creed and left Blake hanging."

"That's enough," Nash said sternly, then offered Gina an apologetic smile. "You'll have to forgive my children. It seems sibling rivalry persists, no matter what their ages."

With the attention now focused on her, Gina felt a blush warm her cheeks. "Uh…I wouldn't know anything about sibling rivalry. I'm an only child."

"An only child?" Eliza repeated, then sighed enviously. "What I wouldn't give to be an only child."

"And miss out on the pleasure of having me as an older brother?" Case teased.

"Yeah, right," Eliza returned wryly, then grinned and blew him an affectionate kiss.

With that, the confrontation was forgotten and the earlier joviality returned, leaving Gina feeling like a ping pong ball as she tried to keep up with all the conversations around her.

While Case dealt with the lock on the door to the loft, Gina thought back over the evening. Throughout dinner she had felt a distinct disadvantage, since everyone gathered for the welcome home celebration had known each other and she'd known only Case. Yet, she couldn't help envying his family's obvious closeness, in spite of the brief confrontation she'd witnessed between Case and Blake.

Remembering the woman who had come to Blake's defense, she tried to recall her name. "Tell me again your half-sister's name," she asked, as she stepped inside the loft.

"Skylar Fortune."

Exhausted both mentally and physically from trying to keep all of Case's family straight in her mind, she stripped off her coat and let it fall to the floor. "Steps, halves and wholes," she said wearily and collapsed onto the sofa. "How on earth do you remember all their names?"

Chuckling, he dropped beside her and cupped a hand at the base of her neck, squeezed. "Years of practice."

She moaned pitifully as he kneaded the tensed muscles of her neck. "Please don't stop," she begged.

The telephone rang, but she ignored it.

"Aren't you going to answer that?" he asked.

She shook her head. "I'm too tired to move. Whoever it is will just have to leave a message."

At that moment, the answering machine clicked on, playing her recorded message. Seconds later, a male voice came through the speaker, "Gina, it's your father. Call me at your earliest convenience."

Ice shot through her veins at the sound of her father's voice.

"Aren't you going to call him back?" Case asked.

She turned her face away. "No."

"But it sounded important."

"I'm not interested in anything he has to say."

"Gina," he scolded gently. "Isn't that rather harsh?"

"Actually I was being kind, considering how I feel about him."

"But he's your father," he reminded her.

"My family's not like yours," she informed him. "My father and I have never been close. His choice, not mine."

He looked at her in puzzlement. "What do you mean, 'his choice'?"

"He never had time for me. Or for my mother, either, for that matter," she added bitterly. "His one and only love is and always has been Reynolds Refining."

She saw the look of surprise on Case's face and felt he deserved some kind of explanation. However she was reluctant to offer one, especially after meeting his family and seeing how close all the Fortunes were. She pushed to her feet and crossed to the window to stare out, needing to distance herself from him, while she shared her less-than-picture-perfect past.

"My mother committed suicide," she said, after a moment. "It was her last and final act to gain my father's attention." She shook her head sadly. "But I'm not sure she gained it even then. I know I never did.

"After her death, he sent me away to boarding school. He rarely called, never came for visits. What communications we did have were filtered through his secretary. She sent my allowance each month, shopped for all my birthday and Christmas gifts and mailed them to me. After boarding school, I went on to college, and the pattern remained the same."

She heard Case rise, felt the weight of his hands on her shoulders, the nudge of his nose against her ear.

"I'm sorry," he said softly.

She blinked back tears at the sympathy in his voice. "Don't be. I'm not. Not anymore."

She stared out the window, remembering the years of neglect, the pain her father had caused her, as well as the means she'd found to finally sever her ties to him completely.

"The only duty he ever felt toward me was a financial one, and when I was a junior in college, I finally found a way to free him of that obligation."

"How?"

"My writing. I was still in college when I sold my first book." She felt the same swell of satisfaction she had the day she'd received the call. "The advance check gave me the financial freedom I needed to cut him out of my life entirely."

"But you moved back to Sioux Falls," he said, obviously wondering why she'd return to the place where her father lived. "Was it in hopes of reuniting with your father?"

"Hardly," she said wryly. "Sioux Falls is home to me, the only one I've never known. He robbed me of that and all that was familiar when he shipped me off to school." She shook her head sadly. "I guess I'm slow, but it took me a while to realize that I had as much right to live here as he did. When I did, I packed up my things and moved back."

"And you haven't seen him since your return?"

"No. In fact, the phone call you just heard was the first time he's attempted to contact me in years."

Finding the entire subject of her father depressing, she turned and forced a smile. "Now that you know all the dirt about my family, how about a glass of wine?"

His gaze on hers, he lifted a hand and brushed her hair back from her face. "I have a better idea."

She shivered as he stroked a thumb beneath her eye. "W-what?"

"This…"

He bent his head and she closed her eyes in anticipation of his kiss. His lips touched hers once, sweetly, withdrew, then touched again. The tenderness in the gesture, the comfort she found in it, drew tears to her eyes. Lifting her arms, she wrapped them around his neck and gave herself up to the kiss, to him.

With a low moan, he vised his arms around, drew her to her toes and deepened the kiss. His taste filled her, a heady aphrodisiac that flowed through her bloodstream and turned her bones to jelly. Everywhere his body touched hers tingled with awareness, anticipation. Need.

His hands seemed to be everywhere at once. Squeezing the cheeks of her buttocks. Sweeping up her back. Framing her face. Her body responded to each and every touch. Arching. Heating. Aching for more. He slid a hand between their chests and covered her breast. Her breath grew ragged, her nipple rigid, as he gently kneaded the mound.

Unable to breathe, to think, she dragged her mouth from his. "Case, please."

He rained kisses over her face, down her neck. "Please, what?"

She knew what it was she wanted from him, what her body ached for. But she knew, too, that she couldn't give in to that need.

She shook her head. "I can't do this."

He drew back far enough to peer at her. "Can't, what?"

"*This*," she said in frustration.

"Why not?"

"I told you before. I'm saving myself for marriage."

"No sex until marriage?" he asked doubtfully. "Isn't that rather extreme?"

"Well, maybe engaged," she conceded reluctantly. "But the commitment has to be there. Commitment is very important to me."

He studied her a moment, then blew out a long breath. "Yeah, I'm sure it is."

"Maybe you should go," she said miserably.

Nodding thoughtfully, he gathered his coat from the chair where he'd dropped it. At the door, he stopped and glanced back. "Gina?"

"What?"

"What kind do you want?"

"What kind of *what*?" she asked in frustration.

"Engagement ring."

"He was kidding," Gina told Zoie the next morning over coffee. "I mean, there was no dropping to one knee, no proposal. He just asked what kind of ring I wanted."

Zoie rolled her eyes. "Girl, you're dumb as a board. If it'd been me, I'd've told him I'd accept nothing less than four carats set in platinum."

"I'm not you," Gina reminded her dryly.

"What's so wrong with marrying Case Fortune?" Zoie asked. "He's easy on the eye, rich as sin. You could do a lot worse, you know."

"I won't marry a man I'm not in love with," Gina stated firmly.

"Why not? Women do it all the time. Who knows? You might even grow to love him over time."

"And I might not," Gina argued, then tossed up her hands. "I don't know why we're even having this conversation. He wasn't serious. It was just a joke."

"How do you know it was? Did he laugh? Crack a smile? Did he say 'gotcha, jokes on you'?"

Gina squirmed uncomfortably in her chair. "Well, no."

"What *did* he do?"

"He just…left."

"Just like that," Zoie said, with a snap of her fingers. "He proposes, then leaves without waiting for an answer?"

Gina slid her spine down the chair, wishing she'd never told Zoie what Case had said. "Well, he kind of hesitated a minute, like he was waiting for me to say something, then he left."

Zoie thumped the heel of her hand against her forehead. "Girl, you are undoubtedly the slowest, most naive woman to ever walk this earth. When a man like Case Fortune even *hints* at marriage, you clamp a ball and chain around his ankle and get him to swear to it in blood, before he can change his mind."

Scowling, Gina rose to dump her coffee down the drain. "I wish I'd never brought it up."

"Who's going to keep you from screwing up your life, if you don't confide in me?"

Gina shot Zoie a frown over her shoulder. "I'm not screwing up my life. I'm merely being cautious."

"Same thing. You've got to learn to take a few risks. Step out on a limb every now and then. That bubble you've been living in might be safe, but it's got to be lonely as hell in there."

"I don't live in a bubble," Gina stated indignantly. "And I'm not lonely. I go out. I have friends."

"Name two," Zoie challenged.

Gina opened her mouth to reply, then closed it, unable to name a single friend, other than Zoie.

"See?" Zoie said smugly. "If I had a good, strong hat pin, I'd pop that bubble and force you out into the *real* world and out of that make-believe one you hide yourself in."

Gina pushed the vacuum around her loft, chasing the dust bunnies that had collected during her week-long creative block. Thankfully, the revisions were now complete and on their way to New York, via Federal Express.

She wished she could pack Zoie up and deal with her as easily.

Flattening her lips, she thrust the vacuum head under the sofa with a little more force than necessary.

"I don't live in a bubble," she grumbled under her breath. Just because her lifestyle was different than Zoie's didn't mean there was anything wrong with it *or* her. Zoie was a free spirit, an adventuress, while Gina enjoyed a quieter, calmer existence.

And she wasn't lonely, she told herself. She wasn't like Zoie, who constantly needed to be surrounded with noise and color, in order to be happy. Gina was perfectly content with her life just the way it was.

Or she had been, until Case came along.

Giving the vacuum an angry shove, she fisted her hands on her hips, as the upright machine went careening across the room and crashed into her dining table. *He* was the problem. Case Fortune. He'd dropped into her world like the proverbial Prince Charming and started making her question everything she'd once held dear.

Mainly, her virginity.

Groaning, she snatched up the stuffed toad from the sofa and flopped down, burying her face in its soft fabric. She'd never considered sex a sport, as did many of her peers. To her, sex was special, sacred, an act two people in love shared exclusively with one another.

If that was true, then why was she always thinking about having sex with Case? she asked herself. She didn't love him. Heck, she barely knew him! So what if his kisses turned her insides to warm butter? Big deal. And who cared if he was drop-dead handsome? In today's world, pretty faces were a dime a dozen. And so what if he did the sweetest, most romantic things? Any man with a finger could punch in a florist's number and order a shipload of flowers. And it certainly didn't take a genius to fold a piece of paper into an airplane and sail it through a window.

But few men did those kinds of things. It took

someone special to even *think* of doing them. Someone thoughtful, kind, generous. Someone with a heart.

She slowly drew the stuffed toad from her face, her eyes wide. Was Case truly the kind of man she'd just described? She racked her brain, trying to think of instances where he'd displayed the traits she'd once attributed to him—cold, heartless, driven.

He had to be all of those things, she told herself. A businessman like Case didn't climb to the position he was currently in without stepping on a few people along the way. Her own father had sacrificed family in favor of business. Surely Case had done the same.

But then she remembered the loving comments he'd made about his mother, while gazing at the portrait of her that hung in his room; his concern for his step-mother when she'd appeared about to faint; the easy camaraderie she'd witnessed between he and his siblings the night he'd invited her to have dinner with his family.

Had she misjudged him? she asked herself honestly. Had she blown any future she might've had with him by refusing to have sex with him?

She firmed her jaw. If so, that was just too bad. Her virginity was important to her, a gift she intended to give to her husband, to the man she loved. If Case wrote her off just because she wouldn't have sex with him, then he wasn't the man for her.

A knock on the door jerked her from her thoughts. Sure that it was Zoie coming to apologize for all the mean things she'd said that morning, she pushed to her feet, thinking she might make her friend squirm for a while before forgiving her. After all, the things Zoie had said were cruel and totally untrue.

But when she opened the door, it was Case, not Zoie, standing in the hallway.

"Case," she said in surprise.

"Are you filming a pancake commercial?" he teased.

Remembering that she had wrapped her hair in a bandanna, she ripped the scarf from her head and balled it into her fist. "Sorry. I was cleaning house."

He lifted a brow. "Aren't you going to invite me in?"

Flustered, she stepped back, allowing him to enter. "Sorry," she murmured as she closed the door behind him.

"That's twice you've apologized in the same number of minutes." He bit back a smile. "Usually that's a sign of a guilty conscience."

She ducked her head, blushing. "More like embarrassment. Obviously, I wasn't expecting company." She peered up at him curiously, suddenly remembering the time. "What are you doing over here at this time of day? Shouldn't you be at the office?"

"I'm playing hooky."

"Really?" she said in surprise. "Somehow you don't seem the type."

"Here we go with that 'type' thing again," he said wearily.

She winced. "Sorry."

"That's three," he said, then smiled, "But you're right. Ordinarily I don't skip out early, but I figured I might as well leave, since I wasn't accomplishing anything, anyway." He gave her a hopeful look. "I was hoping I could talk you into playing hooky with me."

She glanced down at her front and wrinkled her nose at the sight of her faded sweat suit and stocking feet. "I'm not exactly dressed for an outing."

"I was thinking more about a movie marathon." He lifted his briefcase and gave it a pat. "I came prepared with a half dozen DVDs, a box of microwave popcorn and a six-pack of beer."

She choked a laugh. "Are you serious?"

He plopped his briefcase down on the dining table, flipped up the latches and lifted the lid. Inside were a stack of DVDs, as well as the aforementioned boxes of popcorn and six-pack of beer.

"You *are* serious" she said in disbelief.

He shrugged off his coat, then loosened the knot of his tie. "So? What do you say? Are you game for a movie marathon?"

Laughing, she plucked the box of popcorn from the briefcase and headed for the kitchen. "I'll make the popcorn, while you cue up the DVD."

By the time the credits rolled on the last movie, Gina and Case were spooned on the sofa, with Case at her back and one of his legs hooked over hers.

She dabbed a tissue at her eyes. "That movie always makes me cry."

"Me, too."

She snapped her head around to peer at him, then dug an elbow into his ribs. "Liar. You didn't cry."

"I did, too," he insisted.

Picking up the remote, she aimed it at the TV. "Men," she muttered, and turned off the set.

"Just because we don't wear our emotions for all the world to see, doesn't mean we have don't have any."

She shifted to her back to look up at him. "And that's to say that women do?"

He swiped a tear from her cheek and lifted it for her to see. "There's your proof."

Chuckling, she swatted his hand away. "Okay, so I'm a wimp and cry at sad movies."

He bent his head to nuzzle her cheek. "Never argue with me. I'm always right."

She gave his head a playful push. "Your ego is showing again."

He dipped his head over hers. "Let's make out," he whispered against her lips.

Gina knew she shouldn't. Not when she knew what making out might lead to.

But before she could tell him no, he cupped a palm over her breast and her resistance slipped away. Wrapping her arms around his neck, she pulled his face closer.

His kiss seemed to last forever. Little nips of his teeth; deep, greedy thrusts of his tongue. Whispered words that had no meaning, save her name. Hands that stroked and kneaded her breasts. The weight of his leg over hers. The steel-like column of his erection growing against her hip.

Emitting a low groan, he buried his face in the curve of her neck, his breath fanning warm and moist against her skin. He remained in that position for a full minute, before he finally lifted his head with a sigh and met her gaze. "I better go, while I can still walk." He gave her breast a last regretful squeeze and dragged his hand from beneath her sweatshirt. Heaving himself up and over her, he stood, taking a moment to adjust his slacks before turning to face her again.

His smile soft, he leaned down to press a lingering kiss against her lips, then withdrew to meet her gaze. "I'll call you tomorrow," he promised.

Then he was gone.

* * *

Gina had heard the phrase "sexually frustrated" before, but she'd never truly known what it meant…until now. Hours after Case had left and she still burned with need, her body all but aching with it. She couldn't believe Case would arouse her to such a level, then leave without ever attempting to satisfy her—or himself, for that matter. And he'd been aroused, too. She knew, because she'd felt his erection lengthen and harden against her side.

Why hadn't he pressed her to have sex with him? she asked herself in frustration. Hadn't he realized that she was as aroused as he was? That she wouldn't have been able to stop him, even if she'd wanted to? Five more minutes at the mercy of his unbelievable sensual torture, and she would've stripped him naked and had her way with him.

I'm saving myself for marriage.

She rolled to her stomach with a groan and buried her face in her pillow, remembering what she'd told him the previous times he'd attempted to seduce her.

It's all my fault, she thought miserably. By leaving, he was demonstrating his willingness to abide by the rules she'd set. If nothing else, she should admire his nobility.

But acknowledging he was noble didn't take away the ache he'd left her with, *or* the need.

* * *

Across town, Gina's father, Curtis Reynolds, knelt on the kitchen floor, his head gripped between his hands. Dizzy. He was so dizzy. And the pain! It was blinding, debilitating and growing stronger by the day. Unable to sleep, he'd been on his way to the kitchen to pour himself a glass of juice, when the pain had first hit him.

"Mr. Reynolds? Are you all right?"

It took a moment for his housekeeper's voice to penetrate the dark bounds that vised his mind.

He drew in a deep breath, then another, before carefully lifting his head to find his housekeeper stooped over him. "I'm all right, Mary," he assured her.

"Are you sure?" she asked in concern. "I can get you another pain pill, if you want."

He shook his head, as much to clear the webs from it as in response to his housekeeper's question. "No more pills. They muddle my mind."

"But the doctor said—"

"I know what the doctor said," he snapped, then softened the reprimand by giving her hand a reassuring pat. "When a man doesn't have much time left, he should be able to live it with a clear mind, not in a damn fog."

"Let me call Gina," she suggested hesitantly. "If she knew—"

He shook his head. "No. I left her a message

asking her to call and she hasn't. If she came at your request, I'd know it would be out of pity, not because she cared."

"But she's your daughter," she said in frustration. "She should be here with you."

He shook his head sadly. "No. I was never there for her when she needed me. I can't very well ask her to come running just because I need her."

Case had called Gina, as promised, just before noon. After talking for a few minutes, he had invited her to a dinner party at his parents' home. Still suffering the same sexual frustrations that had kept her awake half the night, she'd been tempted to tell him to forget the party and come to her loft instead, as she had different plans for him that night.

Coward that she was, she'd accepted his invitation instead, then prayed that she wouldn't embarrass herself by groping him in front of his family. How could she do anything less, she asked herself, when she'd had nothing but sex on her mind since he'd left her the night before?

Thankfully, selecting the proper outfit consumed most of her afternoon and took her mind off her sexual frustrations. Case had mentioned that it was a black-tie affair, which didn't help at all, as that could mean anything from a cocktail dress to a ball gown, considering the crowd he ran with. Hoping to err on the underdressed side of black-tie, rather than the over, she'd chosen a winter-white pant suit and dressed it up with a pearl-beaded shell to wear beneath the mandarin-style jacket.

She'd spent an hour on her hair, trying to find a style that made her look more glamorous and less like Rebecca of Sunnybrook Farm. Deciding that was impossible, she'd finally swept her hair up in a loose knot and secured it with pearl-studded hairpins.

When Case knocked at her door at precisely seven, she was sliding her feet into heels the same winter-white as her pantsuit. Out of breath—and a whole lot nervous—she hurried to the door.

Her first glimpse of Case nearly brought her to her knees. He was dressed in a dark brown dinner jacket, and had left the collar of his cream-colored shirt open. The contrast in formal versus casual proved devastating to her system, leaving her mouth dry and her speechless.

He gave her a slow look up and down. "Wow. You look like a snow princess."

Pleasure warmed her cheeks. "And exactly what does a snow princess look like?"

He slipped his hands around her waist and clasped them behind her back. "Like something that would melt in my mouth, if I dared taste her." He lifted a brow. "Is there any danger of that happening?"

Emboldened by his appreciative look, she smiled

coyly. "I don't know. I guess you'll have to find out for yourself."

Taking the challenge, he stroked his tongue in a lazy arc over her lips that sent a jolt of desire all the way to her toes.

When he withdrew, she inhaled a ragged breath, then blinked open her eyes. "Did I melt?"

Frowning thoughtfully, he swept his tongue over his lips. "Can't tell. Maybe we should try again."

She pressed a hand against his chest to stop him from kissing her again, fearing that if he did, they'd never make it to his family dinner.

"Maybe we shouldn't," she said with regret. "We don't want to be late."

Five

Gina gave Case's arm a tug, stopping him before he could open the front door of his parents' home.

"Skylar is the one with the long, light brown hair, right?" she asked in a frantic whisper. "Kind of a tomboy?"

"More than kind of. There's nothing frilly or fussy about our Skylar."

"And Eliza has blond hair and blue eyes?"

Chuckling, Case bussed her a quick kiss. "Quit obsessing. No one is going to be offended if you forget his or her name."

His assurance did little to ease Gina's nervousness as she followed him inside.

"Sounds as if everyone is in the den," he said, guiding her in that direction.

Gina's uneasiness increased ten-fold, when she saw the number of people already gathered. Besides the members of Case's family she'd already met, there were some new faces, as well.

Tightening her grip on Case's arm, she nodded toward the fireplace. "Who is that with Maya?" she whispered.

Case followed her gaze. "Her boyfriend, Brad."

Gina watched Maya and Brad for a moment, then lifted her face close to Case's ear. "If Brad's her boyfriend, why does she keep sneaking peeks at Creed?"

Chuckling, Case shook his head. "You women. Always trying to stir up trouble."

"I'm not trying to stir up anything," she said indignantly, then poked her elbow against his ribs and tipped her head discreetly toward the couple again. "See for yourself. She may be talking to Brad, but it's Creed she's got her eye on."

Case followed her gaze and frowned thoughtfully. "It does appear that way," he replied, then shrugged. "It's probably nothing. Come on," he said, drawing her further into the room. "Let's get something to drink."

Though Gina didn't agree with Case's assessment of Maya's covert interest in Creed, she kept her opinion to herself and allowed him to lead her to the bar.

As he handed her a flute of champagne, Eliza joined them, slipping an arm through Gina's. "Better watch him," she warned, eyeing Case suspiciously. "He tries to get women drunk so that he can have his way with them."

Gina blinked, then sputtered a laugh, when she realized that Eliza was teasing her. "Don't worry. I'm wise to his devious ways."

Smiling, Eliza stretched to her toes and planted a kiss on Case's cheek. "Hi, big brother."

He made a show of wiping away her kiss. "Don't try buttering me up now."

Laughing, Eliza caught the hand of a woman passing by and drew her into the group.

"Gina, I'd like for you to meet a friend of mine, Diana Young. Diana, this is Case's current flavor-of-the-month, Gina Reynolds."

"Would you stop?" Case complained. "You make me out to be some kind of playboy." Turning to Diana, he smiled warmly and extended his hand. "It's always a pleasure seeing you, Diana," he said, then shot Eliza a scowl and added, "in spite of the company you keep."

Laughing gaily, Eliza looked around the room. "Quite a crowd, huh?"

Gina followed her gaze and stifled a shudder at the number of unfamiliar faces. "And then some."

"Oh, look!" Eliza cried excitedly. "The Australians have arrived!" She lifted a hand high, catching the attention of the two men who had entered the room and motioned for them to join her.

"You're going to love these guys," she said in an aside to Gina and Diana. "Max is a cousin of ours. Mom and Dad met up with him while they were in Australia and invited he and his business partner, Zack Manning, to visit us in the States. They're interested in horse breeding and want to check out Skylar's setup."

As the men made their way through the crowded room, Gina noticed the recognition that flared in Diana's eyes, as well as the shock.

Eliza caught Max's hand and pulled him into the group. "You already know Case," she said, beginning the introductions. "And this is his date, Gina Reynolds, and this," she said draping an arm at her friend's waist and hugging her to her side, "is Diana Young."

Diana tipped her head in greeting. "Hello, Max."

Max muttered something that Gina couldn't quite hear, then said to the group as a whole, "If you'll excuse me, I need to speak to Patricia and Nash."

Gina watched him stride quickly away, his friend Zack following, and wondered at the odd exchange.

"Let's mingle," Eliza said, and turned away, with her friend Diana in tow.

"That's odd," Gina said, with a frown.

"What's odd?" Case asked.

"Judging by Diana's expression when Eliza first pointed Max out, I would've sworn she already knew him. Yet, they greeted each other as if they were total strangers. And did you notice his expression? He looked almost…angry."

Case reared back to look at her suspiciously. "Are you sure you're a children's author and not a detective? That's two clandestine incidences you've noticed since arriving."

She gave her chin a haughty lift. "Can I help it if I'm more aware of my surroundings than you are? And I was right about Maya," she added stubbornly. "Something is definitely going on between her and Creed."

"Oh really," he said doubtfully.

She tipped her head discreetly toward Creed. "If you don't believe me, look for yourself. Creed's giving Maya's boyfriend the evil eye."

"What?" Case glanced toward Creed. He studied his brother for a moment, then stubbornly shook his head. "He's probably got his mind on something else and is totally unaware of who he's looking at or his expression."

"I don't think so," Gina said doubtfully.

Teasing her with a smile, he leaned close to whisper, "Since you seem determined to stir up a romance, real or imagined, you might want to check out Max's friend, Zack, and Skylar."

Gina scanned the room until she saw the two standing near the doorway, openly flirting. Her eyes shot wide. "Why, they've only just met!" she whispered in return.

Laughing, he slung an arm around her shoulders. "Come on, Super Sleuth. I've got something even more surprising I want to show you."

When he reached the center of the room, he stopped and drew her to his side.

"Could I have everyone's attention a moment?" he called loudly.

Conversations slowly dwindled as people turned to see what was going on.

Uncomfortable at being the center of attention, Gina turned her face against Case's shoulder. "What are you doing?" she whispered frantically. "Everyone's staring."

He looked down at her and smiled. "Of course they are."

"Case…"

Ignoring her pleading look, he turned his attention to the crowd again and directed his next words to them.

"As you all know, family is very important to me. The Fortunes have been blessed with one of massive size, with branches that literally stretch all over the world. Over the years, we've had our share of misfortune, as well as success, and through it all we've stuck together, offering each other whatever support and encouragement was needed at the time. We've laughed together, cried together, and celebrated together.

"Growing up in this house we're gathered in this evening, I've taken part in quite a few celebrations, everything from births to deaths and everything in between. Tonight I'm asking my family and friends to share in a special celebration with me."

A sliver of apprehension snaked down Gina's spine as Case turned to face her. Taking her hand in his, he slipped his other into his jacket pocket, then slowly sank to one knee, pulling out a ring.

Gina gaped, too stunned to speak.

His gaze on hers, he slid the ring onto her finger and said in a voice loud enough for everyone in the room to hear, "Gina Reynolds, would you do me the honor of marrying me and becoming my wife?"

The room was so quiet, she heard the wood shift in the fireplace. Everyone seemed as shocked by Case's proposal as she was. She didn't know what to say. Yes? No? Are you *crazy*?

But he didn't seem to need an answer.

With his gaze on hers, he stood and pulled her into his arms. With everyone in the room watching in shocked silence, he kissed her with a passion that stole her breath.

A single clap of hands sounded, as the guests

slowly absorbed the unexpected announcement. Others gradually joined in, until applause rolled like thunder through the cavernous room.

Case spent the drive home on his cell phone, talking to someone about a business deal that he and Creed were putting together. It wasn't exactly the behavior one might expect from a man who'd just proposed, but it was just as well, because Gina couldn't have carried on a coherent conversation if her life depended on it.

While he conducted business, she sat in the passenger seat of the Escalade, her hands gripped in her lap, her thumb pressed against the ring that circled her finger, still trying to sort through what had just occurred.

Why had he proposed? she asked herself for what seemed like the millionth time since Case had popped the question. He'd never once hinted at marriage, never so much as whispered the words "I love you." They weren't a couple…or at least she'd never considered them as such. The length of their relationship—if one could call it that—certainly didn't lead a woman to expect a proposal. Two weeks was hardly enough time for two people to become acquainted, much less engaged.

She glanced down at her hand and the ring that adorned her left finger. The setting was gorgeous, with rows of baguettes surrounding a huge center diamond. Any woman who received such a stellar engagement ring should be ecstatic, over-the-moon in love.

Gina felt only nausea.

She needed answers, an explanation, but hadn't a clue how to phrase them…or the opportunity to ask them, since the man with the answers was currently on the phone.

Case ended his call just as they stepped into her loft.

Gathering her nerve, she turned to face him and asked the single most question that burned in her mind. "Why did you ask me to marry you?"

He frowned, as if puzzled that she'd ask, then opened his hands. "I'd think that would be obvious."

"Maybe to you it is, but it isn't to me. My, God, Case! We've known each other less than two weeks!"

"I wasn't aware there were time restrictions on how long a man had to wait before proposing."

"That isn't an answer," she said impatiently. "And why did you propose in front of all those people? Everyone was staring at me. It was embarrassing."

His smile indulgent, he crossed to her and caught her hands in his. "Gina, Gina, Gina," he scolded gently. "There was no reason for you to be embarrassed. Those *people,* as you referred to them, are my family and friends. Becoming engaged is a big step, a milestone in my life, in *our* lives. I wanted them present to share in the occasion." He gave her hands a tug, drawing her to him, then released them to wrap his arms around her. "Don't be angry with me, darling." He pressed a kiss against her forehead and her nose, then tipped her face up to his. "I wanted to make this special for you, for us. An event we would always remember."

He tipped her face higher and she watched his face drift down, until his lips touched hers. "Please tell me you're not angry with me," he murmured. "I don't want anything to mar this night." He rained kisses over her face. "Please, Gina," he begged softly.

Weak, she clung to him, all resistance melting from her. "I'm not angry. It's just that…it was so totally unexpected."

He withdrew slightly and caught her left hand. With his gaze on hers, he lifted her hand and pressed his lips against the ring he'd placed there. "Do you like your engagement ring?" he asked.

She shivered, as he stroked his thumb over the back of her knuckles. "I-it's beautiful."

He smiled, as if her response pleased him. "When I saw it, I knew it was meant for you." He slipped his hands inside her jacket and rested them on her shoulders. "Did I tell you that you look beautiful tonight?" he asked softly. He dipped his head to nibble at her throat.

Closing her eyes, she let her head fall back, giving him easier access. "I-I don't remember."

"Then I'll tell you now. You look beautiful." He swept his hands out, easing her jacket over her shoulders. "Gorgeous, as radiant as any bride on her wedding night."

Goose bumps pebbled her flesh as he smoothed his hands down her arms, relieving her of her jacket and letting it fall to the floor in a heap at their feet. Her breath was coming faster and faster, heat danced beneath her skin. She wanted to open her eyes, anchor herself on something substantial to still the dizziness, but her lids were simply too heavy to lift.

She felt his fingers at the back of her neck, heard the soft scrape of her shell's zipper, as he pulled the tab down.

"Case," she said breathlessly. "Stop. Please."

He closed his mouth over hers and peeled the shell from her body, tossed it aside. "There's no reason to stop," he said, nipping at her lips. "We're engaged now. Remember?"

She gulped, remembering she'd told him that she wouldn't sleep with a man until she was married to him, or at the very least engaged.

And, as of three hours ago, she was engaged to Case Fortune.

"Feel this?" he asked, rocking his groin against

hers. "That, my darling, is passion, what you do to me."

A knot twisted in her belly, fear of the unknown. She was grossly inexperienced when it came to sex. Yet, her body responded to his caresses, to the heat that burned between them. Her hands itched to touch him, as he was touching her, to explore his body in the same way he was exploring hers. Her breasts ached for his touch, her lips for his kiss. She wanted him, what pleasure he offered, the secrets he could show her, there was no questioning that.

Growing bold, she slid her hands to his waist and, with trembling fingers, eased his shirttail from his slacks. She felt the quickening of his body as her fingers brushed his skin, the rapid rise and fall of his chest against her breasts.

"I want you in bed," he murmured against her lips and began backing her in that direction as he stripped off his dinner jacket. "I want you naked beneath me, your legs spread beneath mine, your arms around me."

His whispered list of wants made her pulse kick into a faster beat, her womb throb in anticipation. By the time her legs bumped the side of her bed, his jacket and shirt were gone, his chest bare. She gulped, watching, as he unfastened his slacks, pushed them down his legs. His erection pushed at the fly of powder blue boxer shorts.

Swallowing hard, she lifted her gaze to his. "I've never done this before," she said uneasily.

His lips curving in a tender smile, he cupped a hand at her cheek. "Don't worry. I'll teach you all you need to know."

She gulped again, then stepped out of her heels and slacks. Down to her bra and panties, she had to fight the urge to wrap her arms around her middle to cover herself as she watched Case pull back the covers.

When he turned back to her, her heart shot to her throat. His eyes, always a gorgeous blue, seemed to have taken on a darker hue, one that smoldered and burned. He reached out and placed a hand on her cheek. "Make love with me, Gina."

His voice was husky, his touch gentle, as he cupped her face. Helpless to do anything else, she stepped into his embrace, his kiss.

His lips were first soft, then commanding, as he used his chest to force her back on the bed. She felt as if every nerve ending in her body was cued to register each new sensation. The weight of his body sinking against hers, the heat that seeped into her skin, the sweep of his tongue around her mouth. With a hand cupped on her breast between them, he kneaded the mound, making her nipple ache to be touched as well.

Within minutes, she was writhing beneath him, her body demanding a satisfaction she had no idea how to ask for.

"Case," she begged breathlessly. "Please."

"Give me a minute." He rolled off her and stretched to retrieve something from the pocket of his slacks. A condom, she realized nervously, and gulped, as she watched him open the package and slip it into place.

Protected now, he slid a hand down her back and rolled her to her side to face him. With his gaze on hers, he stripped off her panties, then settled his hand between her legs.

She tensed, gasping, as his fingers brushed her center.

"Ssh," he soothed, kissing her. "I won't hurt you. I just want to make sure you're ready."

She nodded, then closed her eyes on a groan, as he began to stroke her, slow, feather-light brushes of his fingers along her femininity. She felt the heat rising deep inside her, the softening of her walls. Fire burned behind her eyes, in her lungs, beneath her skin.

This is torture, was all she could think. The most unbelievable pleasure-evoking, mind-numbing torture she'd ever experienced in her life and she wanted more. She felt the tip of his finger slide inside and tensed against the pressure.

"Relax," he soothed.

His voice became both balm and sorcerer, calming her fears, even as it fanned the flames higher. Her breath grew labored, her womb throbbed for release.

As if sensing her increasing need, he cupped a hand behind her knee and drew her leg over his. "I won't hurt you," he said again, shifting his hips against hers.

Closing her eyes against the heat that threatened to consume her, she nodded.

She felt the nudge of his sex at her opening, and her breath snagged in her lungs.

"Breathe," he urged against her lips. "Just breathe. Let yourself go."

The pressure of his hips against hers increased as he pushed slowly inside. Gasping, desperate to escape this ache that thrummed so deeply inside her, she arched, and he slid a little deeper. One of his hands fanned her buttocks, holding her against him, the other cupped her face. She could feel his breath against her lips, hear the huskiness in his voice, as he murmured words of encouragement.

He inched deeper and met resistance.

"Trust me, baby," he whispered as he clasped her buttocks between his hands. Holding her in place, he pushed his hips forward. She gasped, as pain, red hot and searing, shot through her. A split second later it was gone, giving way to the most incredible flood of sensations.

This is what it means to become one, she thought in wonder, as she struggled to absorb what was happening to her. The most intimate of joinings. Awed by the experience, she opened her eyes, needing to create a visual connection with Case, as well as the physical one they shared, and found him watching her. His face was taut with restraint, his eyes dark with passion. A fine sheen of perspiration beaded his upper lip and his chest. She knew without asking what his self-control was costing him.

Her heart melted at the sacrifice he was willing to make for her, the gentleness with which he had handled her. Looping her arms around his neck, she drew his mouth to hers. "Don't hold back," she whispered against his lips. "Give me everything."

With a groan, he rolled her to her back and surged deeper, his hips pumping against hers in a rhythmic dance Gina found easy to follow. Pressure slowly built inside her, squeezing the breath from her lungs, closing her throat. She felt Case tense, his body going as rigid as steel, the tremble in the legs clamped against hers, the quiver of arms he'd braced at either side of her face.

Eyes now open wide in wonder, she watched the passion build on his face, felt the shudder of release that shook him from head to toe, heard the low growl he emitted and absorbed the sound as he lowered his mouth to hers.

Like a sail that had lost its wind, he sank slowly down over her, with a sigh, and buried his face in the curve of her neck.

"You okay?" he asked softly.

Touched by his concern, it took her a moment to find her voice.

"Yes," she whispered, then wrapped her arms around him and held him close, knowing how inadequate the word was, how incredibly short it fell of describing her true feelings.

With their hearts beating in rhythm, she closed her eyes and slept.

Gina decided she much preferred being awakened by a man than an alarm clock. Butterfly kisses on her eyelids, light strokes of his hands over her belly, whispered words that both seduced and intrigued. Snuggled close against Case's side, she was more than willing to spend the entire day like this.

"Well, well, well."

Gina was so relaxed, so content, it took her a moment to realize that a third person had joined her and Case in her bedroom. When she did, she popped up like a jack-in-a-box to find Zoie standing at the foot of her bed. Mortified that she'd been caught naked in bed with Case, she grabbed the covers and clutched them to her chin.

Case didn't seem to suffer the same embarrassment. He sat up, stretching like a cat.

"Good morning, Zoie."

"Yes it is," she agreed, then dropped her gaze

to the point where the covers gathered loosely at his waist and smiled. "And it's getting better by the minute."

Pursing her lips in annoyance, Gina snatched the covers to hold up high on Case's chest. "You might've knocked first," she snapped irritably.

"I did," Zoie replied, then shrugged. "Guess you couldn't hear it over all the heavy breathing."

Irritated that her friend seemed to be enjoying her discomfort, Gina narrowed an eye at her. "What do you want?"

"Just dropped by to see if it was true," Zoie replied, then grinned. "But I can see that it is."

"What's true?" Gina asked impatiently.

Zoie tossed the newspaper she held onto the bed. "See for yourself," she said, then turned for the door with a casual, "Call me later," tossed over her shoulder.

Her modesty forgotten, Gina snatched up the paper and flipped it open to find the headline Merger Of Fortunes and beneath it read, *Author of children's books pens her own fairy-tale ending*. A stock photo of Case from the newspaper's files was pictured alongside a publicity photo of her. The publicity pic was one her publisher had requested, in which she held a stuffed Timothy Toad at arm length's, her lips puckered, as if she was about to kiss him.

Sickened by the sensationalistic slant to the announcement of their engagement, she shifted her gaze back to the headline. How could Case do this to her? she asked in disbelief. Had he been so sure of her answer, himself, that he would release the news to the paper before he'd even proposed?

"Why?" she cried softly, then turned to him, tears blurring her vision. "How could you do this to me?"

"Do what?" he asked in confusion.

She shoved the paper at him and pushed from the bed. "How could you do such a thing?" she cried. "Is your ego so big you never doubted for a minute that I'd say yes? That no woman would ever say no to the mighty Case Fortune?"

Frowning, Case dragged the paper onto his lap. He swore under his breath as he read the headline, then slapped the back of his hand against the paper. "Do you really think I'm responsible for this?" he asked angrily.

"Well, it certainly wasn't me who leaked the news to the paper! I had no idea you intended to propose last night."

He glared at her a long moment, his jaw clenched, then he heaved a sigh and stretched out a hand. "Come here."

She hesitated a moment, not sure she wanted to touch him. Not after he'd turned their engagement into a media circus.

"Gina," he said firmly.

Though reluctant, she put her hand in his and allowed him to draw her back to bed.

He draped an arm around her and pressed his lips to her hair. "I'm sorry, darling. I know this isn't the way you probably dreamed of having your engagement announced to the world. What woman would? But I didn't leak the news to the paper. I swear, it wasn't me." Sighing wearily, he rested his forehead against her head. "We need to go and see your father. I'm sure he's seen this by now and is probably furious with me for not coming to him first and asking for your hand."

She jerked from his side, her eyes wide in alarm. "No. I don't want to see him."

"But, Gina—"

"No! I don't need his permission to marry. Whatever rights he had in my life he sacrificed a long time ago."

"Okay, okay," he soothed, and drew her back to his side. "We don't have to go and see him."

Blinking back tears, she sat huddled at his side, wishing desperately that she could roll the clock back an hour. Before she'd seen the headlines in the paper, she had been deliriously happy, her heart brimming with her love for Case.

She started at the unexpected thought. *Love?* She slowly relaxed, realizing it was true. She *had* fallen in love with Case. She didn't know the precise moment when her feelings for him had grown to that point, but she knew without a doubt that she loved him.

But did he love her?

"Case?" she asked hesitantly.

"Hmm?"

"Do you love me?"

He drew back to look at her in puzzlement. "Where did that come from?"

Though as frightened to hear his answer as she had been embarrassed to ask the question, she had to know. "You've never said it. I just wondered."

He stared at her a long moment, then smiled and hugged her to his side again. "I'd never marry a woman I didn't love."

Case punched in the security code to his penthouse and strode inside.

"Well, look what the cat dragged in."

He stopped short when he saw Creed stretched out on his sofa, then scowled. "What are you doing here?"

"Just checking on you, big brother. Since you didn't return to the estate last night, I thought you might have stayed here." He gave Case's rumpled clothing a pointed look. "But seeing as how you're wearing the same clothes you had on last night, I assume you spent the night with your new fiancée."

His scowl deepening, Case peeled off his dinner

jacket and tossed it over the back of a chair. "So what if I did?"

Creed folded his hands behind his head. "That was quite a bomb you dropped on us last night."

"Yeah. I imagine it was."

"I knew you were determined to close the deal with Reynolds, but I never dreamed you'd go so far as marry his daughter in order to gain control of Reynolds Refining."

Snorting a laugh, Case stripped off his shirt. "Who said anything about marriage?"

"You did. I heard the proposal myself."

Case dropped his shirt and headed for his bedroom and the bathroom beyond. "There's a mighty big gap between engagement and marriage."

"What?" Creed bolted from the sofa and hurried after him. "Are you saying you don't intend to marry Gina?"

Case twisted on the faucet in the shower. "I won't have to."

Scowling, Creed braced a shoulder against the doorframe. "Maybe you better explain."

"Once Reynolds hears of the engagement—which I assume he has by now, thanks to whoever leaked the story to the newspaper—he'll go along with the merger."

"Why would he do that? He's already told you he's changed his mind."

"His only objection was his desire to leave his daughter a legacy. Since Gina and I are now engaged, there's no reason for him to delay any longer. He gets the money and, by marrying me, his daughter gets the company and the legacy he wanted for her…or so Curtis will think."

Creed held up a hand. "Wait a minute. In order for Reynolds' daughter to obtain partial ownership, the two of you would have to marry."

His smile smug, Case unzipped his fly. "Which is the beauty of my little plan. I don't have to marry her. I just have to make Reynolds think that I am. Once the merger is complete, I'll break the engagement. Dakota Fortunes will own Reynolds Refining and I'll still be a single man."

Creed wagged his head sadly. "Brother, that's low. Even for you."

"Really? I think it's rather magnanimous." Case let his slacks drop and stepped out of them and into the shower. "Gina doesn't want the company. Never has."

"But you proposed to her," Creed reminded him. "I doubt she'll thank you for breaking the engagement."

Case caught the shower curtain in his hand. "Not at first, maybe, but she will eventually. Now, if you'll excuse me," he said and jerked the curtain into place, blocking his brother, as well as the guilt he was trying to heap on him. "I prefer to shower *alone*."

He waited until the bathroom closed behind Creed, then snatched up the bar of soap and began to lather his chest.

Gina *would* thank him, he told himself. She'd never be happy married to a man like him. She was much too sensitive, too…fragile a woman to survive marriage to a man like Case. She needed someone who would dote on her, someone less selfish, less ambitious. Someone who would love her for who she was, not for what she brought to the bargaining table.

Do you love me?

With a groan, he slumped forward, bracing his hands against the tiled wall, hearing again the uncertainty in her voice, the hope, the need, when she'd posed the question. And how had he responded?

He hadn't. He'd cleverly dodged her question, using the evasive tactics he'd honed razor sharp in the business world.

Creed was right, he thought miserably. His treatment of Gina was low, even for him.

While Case was dealing with his guilt, Curtis Reynolds sat at the head of the table in his spacious dining room, reading the morning paper. As usual, he was alone, a fact that had begun to bother him of late.

When he'd first read the morning's headline, he was shocked to discover that his daughter and Case were engaged. But his shock had quickly given way to satisfaction.

About time his daughter married, he told himself, as he sipped his coffee—though, sadly, it was too late for him to gain anything from the union. He would've liked to have had grandchildren. Preferably a boy, but at this point in his life, he would've welcomed a girl.

Reminded of the disease that was quickly eating away at his body and his life, he sat his coffee cup down and sank back in his chair with a weary sigh. Odd how mortality changed a man, he thought glumly. A year ago he wouldn't have given grandchildren a thought. Now that he was facing death, the things he'd once considered so important had lost some of their shine. More and more often he found himself thinking about his wife, his daughter, and the mistakes he'd made with both, rather than the business he'd dedicated his life to building.

Stretching out a hand, he dragged the newspaper from the table and to his lap, the picture of his daughter in full view. She'd developed into a beautiful woman, he thought with a smidgen of pride…and more than a little regret. Not the beauty her mother had been, but an attractive young woman, none the less.

How long had it been since he'd seen her last? he wondered. Ten years? Probably closer to twelve.

The summer before she began college, she'd made a brief visit home. He remembered the visit well. The flash of temper she'd displayed when he'd told her he was leaving on a business trip the day after her arrival. But he'd seen hurt in her eyes, as well. The disappointment. And that's the memory that haunted him now.

It hadn't at the time, he thought sadly. He'd dismissed the guilt, just as he had each time he'd witnessed similar reactions from his wife. He'd done so by telling himself that his business was important, that all the time he spent building Reynolds Refining was for his family, his wife and daughter. Hadn't he provided them a cushy life? A regal home, a respected place in society, the finest of everything money could buy?

But now that he was facing his mortality, he realized the mistakes he'd made, all that he'd lost, just as his wife had tried to tell him so many times in the past. He was fifty-seven years old, still young really, but alone in the world. He'd driven his wife to suicide by allowing his ambition to supercede her needs and destroyed whatever chance he might've had at a relationship with his daughter.

And for what? he asked himself in frustration. A damn company. Earlier that week, he'd heard a Country Western song on the radio that pretty well capsulized the lesson he'd learned. The guy had been singing something about there not being any luggage racks on a hearse.

How true, he acknowledged sadly. He'd dedicated his life to building and collecting *things*. And now that he was facing the end of his life, he realized the mistakes he'd made, the lives he'd damaged, all he'd lost. In chasing the illusive rainbow of success, he'd sacrificed what was most important.

Family.

He dropped his head back against the chair with a sigh. For a man who'd spent the majority of his life alone, he'd never once suffered loneliness.

But now that he was facing death, it seemed loneliness was his constant companion.

Six

Case spent hours trying to think who could have leaked the story of his engagement to the newspaper and couldn't come up with a single person on whom to pin the blame. He hadn't told anyone his plans, not even Creed, the one person he'd shared every dark and dirty secret of his life and had since they were in diapers together. He hadn't confided in his brother because he'd known Creed would've tried to talk him out of proposing to Gina. Creed would have insisted that Reynolds Refining wasn't worth Case sacrificing his freedom for, that it was wrong to use Gina in such a selfish way. It just proved how well he knew his brother, because Creed had hit him with both points.

The same guilt that had slammed Case while he was in the shower tried to land on him again, but he quickly shrugged it off, telling himself that all's fair in love and war. And this was definitely war. Reynolds had drawn the line himself, when he'd balked on going through with the merger.

And speaking of Reynolds.... By now Curtis would've either read the news or heard about the engagement from some gossip. Although Case's initial reaction to seeing the headlines had been a desire to black the eye of the person who had leaked the story of the engagement, it hadn't taken him long to realize that the leak was probably to his advantage. Especially since Gina refused to go with him to talk to her father.

But he'd still like to know who was responsible for the leak. When his name made the news, he preferred to choose how and when it appeared himself.

As Case approached Creed's office, he heard voices inside and stopped, thinking he'd come back later when Creed was alone. But then he recognized the voice as that of his step-brother, Blake, and continued on.

"You know how mother is," Blake was telling Creed. "She's always got one man or another on a string."

"But Phillip Gaddis has got to be a good twenty years older than Trina," Creed said in amazement.

"Since when has age stopped Mom?" Blake said dryly. "Not when the guy has money. I'd imagine all the jewelry Gaddis gifts her with makes up for any areas where he might fall short."

Anger burned through Case's veins, as the pieces to the puzzle finally fell into place. It was Trina Watters Fortune, Blake's mother and Case's *ex*-step-mother, who had leaked the news of the engagement to the paper.

Case had bought Gina's ring at Gaddis' jewelry store, and must have mentioned Gina's name during the transaction. Whether by accident or design, Gaddis had then told Trina about the purchase. Conniving shrew that she was, Trina had run straight to the paper with the news, hoping to cause trouble for the Fortunes, which seemed to be her favorite pastime.

He stormed into Creed's office, smoke all but coming out his ears as he bore down on Blake. "You tell that bitch of a mother of yours to keep her nose out of my business."

Startled, Blake glanced over his shoulder, then slowly rose, his eyes narrowed in anger. "You have no right to call my mother a bitch."

Case lifted a brow. "Don't I?" He poked a stiff finger against Blake's chest. "Listen to me, little brother, and listen good. Your mother has stirred up trouble for the Fortunes her last time. If she so much as *speaks* a Fortune's name, I'll personally kick her ass so far out of this town, she won't be able to find her way back to Sioux Falls."

"Why you—" His face red with fury, Blake reared back to punch Case.

Creed quickly stepped between the two, catching Blake's fist in his own, before it hit its target. "Hold on there, Blake," he warned.

His eyes blazing with anger, Blake yanked free. "I'm not going to stand here and let him talk about my mother that way."

"No," Case informed him. "You're going to leave this building and go directly to your mother's and tell her exactly what I said. She's the one who leaked my engagement to the press, which makes her a troublemaker in my book, as it wasn't her news to share."

Feeling a bit better after having had his say, Case gave the cuffs of his dress shirt a smart tug, then turned to leave. "Don't take this personally, Blake," he tossed over his shoulder. "It's your mother who's the problem."

Surrounded by Tululah, Timothy, Tyrone and Tessa, her toad friends, Gina held her left hand out before her face.

"What do you think, Timothy?" she asked

thoughtfully, as she studied the ring, then wrinkled her nose. "You're right. It is kind of big."

She turned to Tululah, Toadsville's resident vamp, as if Tululah had spoken. "Well, of course *you* would like it," she told the voluptuous toad, then gave her a chiding look. "Now don't be jealous, Tululah. Green is such an unflattering color on you."

Laughing gaily, she scooped Tululah up and kissed her full on her painted toad-lips. "Can you believe it?" she cried. "I'm getting married! *Me,* poster girl for Wallflowers Anonymous, is really getting married!" Humming the wedding march, she waltzed Tululah around the room. "Of course you can be my maid of honor," she said, as if replying to a question Tululah asked.

She resumed her humming, but slammed into an unexpected wall of resistance. Swaying to a stop, she found Zoie standing opposite her, scowling, her arms folded across her chest.

Embarrassed at being caught dancing with a toad, she tucked Tululah behind her back. "Zoie," she said meekly. "I didn't hear you come in."

Her scowl deepening, Zoie plucked Tululah from behind her back and tossed the stuffed animal onto the sofa with the other toads. "Sorry to break up the family celebration," she said dryly, "but you were supposed to call me."

Gina winced. "Oops. Sorry. I forgot."

Taking Gina firmly by the arm, Zoie marched her to the dining table. "And here I thought I thought I was your best friend."

Gina sat down hard in the chair Zoie had shoved her onto and blinked up at her friend in surprise. "You *are* my best friend."

Pouting, Zoie slumped down in the chair opposite her. "Then how come Tullulah gets to be your maid of honor?"

Gina choked a laugh. "Are you serious? Tullulah can't serve as my maid of honor. She's a stuffed animal!"

Zoie made a show of wiping perspiration from her forehead. "And all this time I thought I was living next door to a loft full of live toads."

Her nose in the air, Gina pushed up from her chair to fetch the coffee pot. "Better be nice to me," she warned as she poured them both a cup, "or I *will* ask Tullulah be my maid of honor."

Dropping the spurned-friend-act, Zoie scooted closer to the table and looked expectantly at Gina when Gina sat back down. "So it's true? Case really asked you to marry him?"

Feigning nonchalance, Gina fanned the fingers of her left hand over the table. "I don't know. You tell me."

Zoie's eyes bugged. "Whoa, baby! Would you

get a load of that rock?" She grabbed Gina's hand to examine the ring more closely. "That's gotta be at least four carats."

Gina fluttered her fingers just to watch the diamonds sparkle. "I wouldn't know, but it's a gorgeous ring, isn't it?"

"Honey, that's not a ring, that's a 401-K, a retirement account. A friggin' lottery win! Did you pick it out?"

Her smile dreamy, Gina drew her hand back to admire the ring again. "No. Case did."

"Looks and taste, too." Zoie heaved a sigh. "Some girls have all the luck."

Laughing, Gina picked up her coffee cup and took a sip.

"So when's the big day?" Zoie asked.

"We haven't set one, yet."

"What are you waiting for? Nail him down, girl! Don't take a chance on him skipping out on you."

Gina's smile slipped a bit at the possibility, but she quickly pushed it back into place. "He only proposed last night. There's time yet."

Zoie leaned forward, her eyes sparkling with excitement. "Speaking of last night, how is he in bed?"

Unaccustomed to speaking so openly about sex, Gina dropped her gaze, blushing. "Okay, I guess."

"Just *okay*?"

Trying her best not to grin, Gina peeked up at her

friend from beneath her lashes. "He's good. *Really* good. Off the charts, mind-blowingly fantastic."

"Hoo-hoo!" Zoie hooted, waving her arms above her head. "I knew it! God wouldn't give a man that kind of body without the skill to use it."

After lunch, Case stopped by his secretary's desk before heading into his own office.

"Anything needing my attention, Marcia?"

"Mail came while you were gone." She picked up a stack of envelopes from her desk and handed it to him. "And Curtis Reynolds called."

Case lifted a brow, surprised to hear from Gina's father so soon. "Am I supposed to call him back?"

"No. I asked, but he said for me to just tell you he's having his lawyer resume work on the merger."

It was the response Case had hoped for, gambled his bachelorhood on.

But, for some reason, the elation he'd expected didn't come.

"Hold my calls, will you?"

"Well, sure," she replied, obviously surprised by the request, then looked at him curiously. "Are you okay?"

He shrugged and turned for his office. "I'm fine."

But he wasn't fine, he thought, as he closed the door behind him. He should be elated, punching his fist in the air in a sign of victory at his success in outsmarting Reynolds. Instead, he felt…what? Depressed? Guilty?

Grimacing, he tossed his mail on his desk, then sank down in his chair and dropped his head back to stare at the ceiling. He shouldn't feel depresssed or guilty, he told himself. He should be elated. Curtis had resumed the paperwork on the merger, which should make Case happy, since that was what he had wanted and schemed for from the beginning. And he'd gotten Curtis's cooperation without having to sacrifice his bachelorhood.

So why the hell wasn't he cracking open a bottle of champagne and toasting his success with Creed?

Because of Gina, you idiot.

Case tensed as his conscience's repsonse. Gina? he asked himself.

Yeah. Gina. Have you consisdered her feelings in any of this? You can't just dump her because Curtis had agreed to the merger. You'll break her heart! Hasn't she suffered enough heartbreak in her life without having to add you to the list?

Case gulped, imagining Gina's reaction when he broke their engagement. She'd take it hard, there was no doubt about that. But all's fair in love and war, he reminded himself. She'd get over it. Probably be better off without him, considering the differences in their personalities and goals.

Maybe. Maybe not. But what about you? How

are you going to get over her? She's gotten under your skin, hasn't she? Carved herself a niche in your heart?

Case stiffened at the suggestion. No way, he told himself. His relationship with Gina was nothing more than a business deal, and he'd learned early on never to allow his emotions to get involved where business was concerned.

That may have been true in the past, but not anymore. Admit it, Case. You've fallen in love with her.

Case sat bolt upright. Love? Hell, he wasn't in love with Gina! Sure, he liked her well enough. She was funny in a quirky sort of way, and for a rank beginner, she was damn good in bed. And he enjoyed spending time with her. She was easy to get along with, interesting to talk to. But love? He shuddered at the thought. No way.

Then why aren't you cracking open the champagne over the resumption of the merger? I'll tell you why. Because you know the game's over. You don't need Gina any longer. It's time to get rid of her. But let me tell you something, buddy. Once she learns how you used her, she isn't going to want you, *either.*

A hole opened in Case's gut as he tried to imagine his life without Gina in it. He didn't want to hurt her, and he sure as hell didn't want her hating him. Surely there was a way they could end things and still be friends.

But how?

His conscience, which he hadn't been able to silence only moments ago, suddenly went mute.

There was a way, he told himself stubbornly. He'd finessed his way out of tougher situations and come out on top. And he would with this one, too.

Gina couldn't help herself. The smile she'd worn since Zoie had left seemed perpetually glued to her face. In spite of her euphoric mood, she'd worked most of the day on an idea for a new book.

Or tried to.

At odd moments, she would catch herself daydreaming about Case and filling page after page, practicing writing her married name: Mrs. Chase Fortune. Gina Reynolds Fortune. Gina Fortune. To be honest, the pages bearing her married name far outnumbered the manuscript pages she'd produced.

But what difference did it make? she asked herself. It wasn't as if she had a pressing deadline. Besides, she was getting married! A bride-to-be was entitled to twiddle away a day in total bliss.

But just one, she told herself sternly. She still had a book to write and illustrate, as well as a wedding to plan. She would need to talk to her agent and her editor, request an extension on the deadline for her next book. She didn't want any distractions or added stress. Planning a wedding took a lot of time. A bridal gown and bridesmaid dresses to shop for. Flowers and music to select. Caterers to interview, a menu to decide upon. Reception locations to be scouted. So many decisions to be made!

Her excitement slowly faded as she realized she'd be making those decisions alone. She had no mother to advise her or assist with the plans.

And no father to give her away.

She pushed slowly away from her computer and moved to stare out the wall of windows that overlooked the street below, unexpected tears blurring her vision. A wedding was one of the biggest milestones in a woman's life, something her entire family should share in.

But Gina had no family. No mother, no siblings. And she had severed ties with her father. Glancing over her shoulder at the phone in the kitchen, she caught her lower lip between her teeth. She could return his call, attempt to reestablish a relationship with him.

She whipped her head around to face the window again. She wasn't calling him, she thought stubbornly. Why should she invite him to share in this special time with her, when he'd abandoned her when she'd needed him most?

As she stared out the window, a new worry surfaced to push the thoughts of her father from her mind. Who would she invite to the wedding? Traditionally, the church was divided into two sections: friends of the bride, and friends of the groom. Case would have tons of people to fill his side of the church, but who would sit on her side?

That worry quickly morphed into another. What if Case wanted several attendants to stand with him? She had only Zoie.

Panic rose slowly, as she envisioned a church packed with guests, their attention focused on the ceremony being conducted at the altar. She shivered, all but able to feel the intensity of the gazes fixed on her back. She hated crowds, hated even more being the center of attention.

A knock at the door had her whirling from the window, her heart racing.

"Gina?"

At the sound of Case's voice, she ran to throw open the door.

"Can we elope?" she begged desperately.

He blinked at her in surprise, then brushed past her, stripping off his coat. "Where did *that* come from?"

She closed the door and turned for the sofa, wringing her hands. "I've been thinking about the wedding and I realized that I don't have anyone to give me away."

"You have a father," he reminded her.

She burned him with a look.

He held up his hands. "Forget I said that."

Moaning pitifully, she flopped down on the sofa. "Even if I was willing to ask him to give me away, I wouldn't have anyone to invite to a wedding."

He sat down beside her and cupped a hand behind her neck. "Of course you do," he assured her.

"I don't!" she cried.

"Come on, Gina," he scoffed. "You went to college, didn't you? Surely you made a few friends while you were there."

"With a mother who committed suicide and a father who never came for visits?" She shook her head. "It was easier to be alone, than have to answer a zillion questions."

When he said nothing in response, she turned to look at him. "Couldn't we just elope?" she asked hopefully. "Please?"

His smile soft, he gave her neck a reassuring squeeze. "Let's not worry about this right now. We'll plan on having a long engagement. As long as you want. That'll give you time to decide exactly the kind of wedding you want."

She flung her arms around his neck. "Thank you, thank you, thank you!"

He pulled her onto to his lap and nuzzled his nose at her neck. "If you really want to thank me, I know a better way."

Gina might not have had much sexual experience

prior to the previous night she'd spent with Case, but she considered herself an exceptionally fast learner. Shifting to straddle him, she nipped at his lips. "Does it start something like this?" she asked suggestively.

Gina considered it amazing how much one single act could change a person's life. Since becoming engaged to Case, her social life had gone from turtle-pace-dull to rabbit-run-exciting in the blink of an eye. In a four-day span, she'd attended a banquet at the Sioux Falls' Chamber of Commerce honoring its new members, a cocktail party to celebrate a friend of Case's promotion to president at the bank where he worked and had lunch with his sister Eliza. Besides the social outings, she'd spent countless hours alone with Case.

And those were the best, she thought giddily. She'd never known that kissing and cuddling could be such fun. And the sex…. Well, it was more than fun. It was fantastic! Much better than she'd even imagined.

She considered it amazing, too, for someone who had always lived alone, how quickly she'd adapted to having Case around all the time. When he wasn't at his office, he was at her loft. He slept with her, ate breakfast with her before leaving for work, then returned to her loft in the afternoon. So far, she hadn't been required to prepare anything more than a simple breakfast for him, but since he hadn't mentioned any commitments for that evening, she had decided it was time to show off her culinary skills. She didn't want him thinking he'd chosen a wife who didn't know how to cook!

She'd selected an Italian theme for their dinner, and had a pan of lasagna baking in the oven, a salad chilling in the refrigerator and a bottle of wine open on the table she'd set for two. She folded foil around the garlic bread waiting to be popped into the oven, then turned to admire the table she'd set, pleased with her efforts.

The grate of a key signaled Case's arrival and she quickly hurried to the door to greet him.

Rising to her toes, she planted a kiss on his lips, then sank back to her heels and smiled. "Hi."

"Hi, yourself." He lifted his nose to sniff the air as he shrugged out of coat. "Is that spaghetti I smell cooking?"

She took his coat and hung it in the entry closet. "No. Lasagna. I hope you like it."

"If it tastes as it good as it smells, I know I will."

"Hopefully it does." She led the way to the kitchen. "Would you like a glass of wine while the bread bakes?"

He took the bottle from her. "Why don't I pour while you take care of whatever needs tending in the kitchen?"

Pleasure all but oozed from her as she surrendered the bottle to him and left him to pour their wine. She liked this sharing of duties, she thought, as she slid the bread into the oven alongside the lasagna. The comradery, as well as the ease she felt in his presence. Case wasn't perfect. She'd be the first to admit he had his faults. He was a bit cocky at times—okay, a whole lot cocky, she conceded. And he could be overbearing, too. But he could also be thoughtful and considerate, two traits she hoped to nurture as they spent more time together.

She was pulling the salad bowl from the refrigerator, when she felt his breath on the back of her neck. She closed her eyes and inhaled deeply. She loved the smell of him, the grate of his beard against her skin as he pressed his lips against the base of her neck. Her smile deepening, she turned and kissed him fully, before taking the wine glass he offered.

"So how was your day," she asked, leading the way to the living room.

"Busy. Meetings mostly. Contracts that needed my attention. That kind of thing. Nothing earth-shattering." He sat down on the sofa and stretched out his legs, while she popped a CD in the player and adjusted the sound. "How was yours?"

"I had lunch with Eliza. She asked where we were planning to live, after we're married."

"What did you tell her?"

Lifting a shoulder, she sat beside him, drawing her feet beneath her. "Since we haven't discussed it, I told her I didn't know." She paused to take a sip of her wine, silently praying he wouldn't want to live at the Fortune estate with all the family, as he did now. She really liked his family, but she couldn't imagine the two of them ever enjoying the same privacy the loft offered them "We could live here," she suggested hesitantly. "There's plenty of space. We could even remodel, if you wanted."

He gave her knee an indulgent pat, then tipped his head back against the sofa and closed his eyes. "No need to rush into making any decisions. We've got lots of time."

Disappointed that he hadn't leaped at her suggestion, she took another sip of her wine. "You like the loft, don't you?" she asked, after a moment.

He opened one eye to peer at her. "Of course I do. Why do you ask?"

She lifted a shoulder. "I don't know. I guess I was hoping we could live here."

He closed his eyes again. "Like I said, we've got lots of time to decide things like that."

Though unsatisfied with his answer, she laid her head on his shoulder, knowing that he was right. They had plenty of time to decide where they wanted to live. Content simply to be with him, she closed her eyes, too, and let the soft music wash over her.

The phone rang, it's loud sound jarring her from her relaxed state. With a groan, she unfolded her legs and hurried to the kitchen, wanting the accessibility the extension offered so she could check on the bread.

"Hello?" she said as she opened the oven door and peeked inside.

"Is this Gina Reynolds?"

She frowned, not recognizing the woman's voice. "Yes. This is Gina."

"I'm so sorry to call you so unexpectedly like this, but I felt you should know."

"Know what?" Gina said suspiciously. "Who is this?"

"I'm sorry." The woman sounded sincerely contrite, if a bit frazzled. "I'm Mary Collier, your father's housekeeper."

Gina flattened her lips, thinking it would be just like her father to ask someone to contact her, rather than do it himself. Every birthday present she'd received since her mother's death and every letter had been filtered through his secretary. "Did he ask you to call me?" she asked irritably.

"No, dear, he didn't. I'm sorry to have to tell you this, but your father passed away this afternoon."

Ice slid through Gina's veins. Numb, she stood motionless, feeling as if the air had been sucked from the room, making it difficult to breathe. "Dead?" she whispered, then pressed a hand to her lips, to smother the whimper that pushed at her. "But…how?"

"He's been ill for a month or more," Mary said quietly, then sniffed, obviously having a difficult time with her own emotions. "Cancer. By the time the doctors determined that it had originated in his brain, his body was covered with it. There was nothing they could do for him. Nothing at all."

Gina sank weakly to the floor, the phone clutched to her ear. "Surely there was something. Radiation? Chemotherapy? Something!"

"No, dear, I'm sorry. The cancer was too far gone for any type of treatment. The best the doctors could do for him was prescribe morphine to help him deal with the pain."

Gina dropped her forehead to her palm, trying to fight her way through the shock, the realization that her father was gone. "What do I need to do?" she asked quietly.

"Nothing. He made all the arrangements himself. He left his instructions both with his lawyer and the funeral home. Mr. Andrews, the director of the funeral home, should be calling you shortly to go over the details of his last requests, as well as give you the date and time of the service. But I thought I should call you first. Give you some warning. I imagine this comes as quite a shock."

Gina nodded numbly. "Yes. Yes, it does."

"Well, I guess I should go now. If you need anything, anything at all, call me. I live at your father's house. Or I do for the time being. You can reach me on the main number."

"Yes. I will. Thank you, Ms. Collier."

Gina punched the button to disconnect the call, then pulled her knees up and dropped her head to rest on them. *He's gone,* she thought, having a difficult time accepting the realization. *My father's gone.*

"Gina?"

She looked up to find Case standing over her, his forehead creased in concern.

He sank to a knee and placed a hand on her shoulder. "Are you okay?"

Tears welled in her eyes, filled her throat. She shook her head, momentarily too choked by emotion to speak. "It-it's my father." She hiccuped a sob and looked up at him. "He's dead, Case. My father's dead."

Gina wasn't sure how she made it through the past few days. Viewing the body. The visitation. The funeral. Without Case beside her, she doubted she would have survived the ordeal. He'd stood like a rock at her side, gently guiding her through each formality, acting as a buffer between her and all those who came to offer their condolences. Physically supported her, as she'd watched her father's casket lowered into the ground. All the while she was grieving, he'd never once reminded her of her refusal to return her father's phone call, or thrown in her face her claim to have severed all ties with her father. He didn't have to. Gina had lived with those regrets every minute of every day since receiving the news of his death.

The irony of the situation didn't escape her. She'd spent years convincing herself she hated her father, resenting him for the total disregard with which he'd treated both her and her mother. The only thing she'd ever wanted from him was his love, and now that he was gone, she realized she'd never have the chance to experience it. She agonized over all the wasted years, blaming herself for allowing her anger and resentment to keep her from what she'd always claimed she wanted and needed most.

Her father.

Seven

Dreading the upcoming meeting with her father's attorney, Gina remained silent as she and Case rode the elevator down to the garage of her building.

"If you want, I can go with you," he offered. "I can have my secretary cancel my appointments."

That he would put her needs before his own touched her in a way that nothing else could. "There's no need for you to change your plans," she assured him. "Like I told you, this is just a preliminary meeting. It shouldn't take long."

As they stepped off the elevator, he stopped and pulled her coat snuggly around her, buttoned it up. "Are you sure?" he asked again. "I really don't mind."

Grateful for his concern, she wrapped her arms around him and laid her cheek against his chest, knowing she'd need the strength she drew from him to make it through the appointment, no matter how brief. "I'll be fine," she said again, then stepped back and gave him a brave smile. "Really. I'll be fine."

Draping an arm over her shoulders, he walked her to her car. "Call me when you're done. If it's around noon, maybe we can squeeze in lunch before you head back home."

"Sounds good."

He dropped a kiss on her cheek, then turned for his own car. She watched him walk away, grateful for the comfort and support he'd given her during the week following her father's death.

"Case?"

He stopped and glanced back over his shoulder.

She hesitated, wanting to tell him how much he meant to her, how much she appreciated all he'd done for her. But the only words that came out were, "I love you."

Sitting opposite Gina at a conference table, Bill Cravens, senior partner in Cravens, Conners and O'Reilly Law Firm, passed Gina a thick sheaf of papers, then adjusted his own copies of the documents in front of him.

"Your father was a meticulous businessman," he began, "which will certainly facilitate the transfer of property and the probation of his will."

Unsure how she was expected to answer, Gina nodded.

"I don't want to embarrass you in any way or cause you discomfort, but I think it's important that you know that I'm aware of the rift between you and your father."

She dropped her gaze, ashamed of the part she'd played in widening that rift.

"I was more than your father's attorney," he said kindly. "I was his friend and have been for more years than I can count. Though I loved Curtis dearly, he wasn't without his faults. Most pertained to his personal life.

"He wasn't a selfish man, though you have every right to believe he was. Curtis grew up in poverty. His childhood was anything but desirable, yet he came out of it with two distinct goals. The first was to amass wealth, which, without question, he accomplished. The second was to see that his family never suffered as he had.

"Unfortunately, in striving to achieve his goals, he denied his family what they needed and wanted most. *Him.* His time, his attention. I was aware of this, as were most of his friends. I tried to talk to him about it on several occasions." He shook his head sadly. "But Curtis wouldn't listen, refused to see his ambition as a fault. Your mother...he broke her heart. She loved him more than life itself, which she later proved. He loved her, too, yet she could never reach him, was never able to make him understand that she needed him more than she did the baubles he bought for her."

Tears burned in Gina's eyes, her throat. She'd witnessed enough of her parents' marriage to know that what Mr. Cravens said was true.

"Regrettably, being diagnosed with cancer was what finally got through to him, brought about the change. If I hadn't witnessed the transformation myself, I would never have believed it possible. When faced with his own mortality, Curtis finally realized the mistakes he'd made, all he'd lost."

He paused and drew a single sheet of paper from the folder at his side. "He gave this to me," he said, pushing the page across the table to Gina. "Asked me to give it to you."

Gina glanced down and saw that it was a letter, written in her father's own handwriting. She glanced up at Mr. Cravens in question.

He leaned back in his chair and waved a hand. "Go on and read it," he suggested. "It might help you better understand his state of mind at the time of his death, the changes he'd undergone."

Gulping, Gina picked up the letter and began to read.

Dear Gina,
By the time you read this letter, I'll be gone. I don't say that to be morbid or in an effort to win your sympathy. It's simply a fact.

I want you to know that I don't blame you for cutting me out of your life. You have every right to hate me. I wasn't a very good father. I never gave you the time or attention you deserved and needed. But I want you to know that it wasn't because I didn't love you. I do and always have. I just lacked the ability to show you in the proper way.

It saddens me that I won't live long enough to see you marry, to hold the children you and Case will have someday. It saddens me more to know that I won't have the opportunity to tell you how wrong I was, to make up to you for all the times you needed me and I wasn't there. Believe me when I say, the greater loss is mine.

You've grown into a beautiful woman and one who makes me very proud. Who would have ever thought the stuffed toad I gave you when you were a little girl would lead to you becoming a successful writer? Not that I'm trying to take credit for your success. I'm not. You earned that in your own right and without my help.

I take with me to my grave a bushel load of regrets. The greatest is the way in which I failed you and your mother. In spite of what you might think, I loved your mother. And I love you, Gina. I always have. If you remember nothing else about me, please remember that.

Dad

Sniffling, Gina carefully folded the letter, sniffled again, as she tucked it into her purse. If she'd felt guilty before, her father's last words set that guilt in stone that weighed heavily on her heart. He'd loved her. Her father had loved her. If only she'd returned his call, she thought miserably. Maybe they could've re-established their relationship, built it into something lasting, a memory she could treasure in the years ahead.

"Don't."

She glanced up to find Mr. Cravens looking at her, his eyes soft in compassion.

"I know what you're thinking," he said. "You're blaming yourself for all the lost years. But Curtis wouldn't want that. That is precisely why he wrote the letter. He wanted you to know that he takes full responsibility for the breach in your lives. He wanted, too, for you to know that he loved you. In spite of his actions, his lack of attention, he truly loved both you and your mother."

His assurance released something inside Gina and a warmth that could only be explained as her father's love slowly spread through her chest. Overcome with emotion, she could only nod.

Mr. Cravens cleared his throat and pushed the papers in front of him into a neater stack. "Now, let's get down to the business at hand," he suggested.

Gina dabbed at her eyes, then focused her gaze on the document in front of her.

"The most important matter we need to discuss this morning," he informed her, "is the future of Reynolds Refining."

She panicked, thinking Cravens expected her to take over the reins of her father's company. "But I don't know anything about running a refinery."

He laughed softly. "I didn't expect you would. Thankfully your future husband *does*. Curtis was unable to complete the merger of Reynolds Refining with Dakota Fortunes before he died, but we can rectify that easily enough, as your father authorized your signature on the document, in the event of his death."

Gina blinked in confusion, trying to make sense

of what Mr. Cravens was telling her. "I'm sorry. I don't understand."

He gestured to the documents in front of her. "If you'll take a look at the third set of papers, they are the ones pertaining to the merger."

Gina flipped through the stack and pulled out the document he mentioned. She quickly flipped through the pages, but the legal jargon made no sense to her. At the bottom of the last page, her gaze locked on the name "Case Fortune."

Case hadn't said anything about being involved in a merger with her father, she thought in growing confusion. Never once had he mentioned doing any business at all with her father! She glanced at the date below Case's name and saw that it coincided with the day their engagement had appeared in the newspaper. A knot of dread twisted in her belly.

Keeping her expression free of the doubts that filled her mind, she looked up at Mr. Cravens. "Was it because of the cancer?" she asked. "Is that why my father decided to sell the company?"

He gave her a strange look. "Well, no. How could it, when the negotiations began months ago? Of course, Curtis backed out on the deal the first time around, when he learned he had cancer. He decided he wanted to leave the company to you as a legacy, instead." He shot her a wink. "Then you surprised us all by becoming engaged to Case. No one was more surprised by the news than Curtis. *Or* more pleased, I might add. With you marrying Case, leaving you a legacy was no longer a concern for him. As Case's wife, by law you would own half of all that is his, including Reynolds Refining, which provides the legacy your father had wanted for you."

Numb, Gina stared at the document again, her heart fighting what her mind was telling her was true. Case had used her. In order to gain control of her father's company when Curtis had backed out on the deal, he'd grasped at the only means her father had left him. Marry the owner's daughter.

She rose, a hand pressed to her stomach. "I'm sorry, Mr. Cravens. We'll have to finish this another time. I'm not feeling well."

It wasn't a lie, Gina told herself, as she rushed from the conference room.

She had never felt more sick in her life.

Gina left Cravens office, anxious to return home and bury herself in the one spot where she felt safe. Her loft.

But instead of turning right in the direction of her building, she made a left and headed out of town. She hadn't driven on this road in years. Had avoided it at all costs. It was the road to her father's house.

She parked on the driveway in front of the house

and, for a moment, just stared, allowing the memories to wash over her.

The house had changed little over the years. It still appeared huge, even when looked at through adult eyes, rather than those of a child. It wasn't the only home her parents had lived in as husband and wife, but it was the last.

When her father had worked with the architect to design it, he'd been determined to create a structure that would reflect his success, his current station in life. Three stories high, it was constructed of antique brick and trimmed in a soft cream paint. Tall, dark green shutters flanked the French doors that opened from both the living room and dining room onto a wide veranda that formed a half-moon veranda on the front of the house. She remembered, as a little girl, running the invisible circle the doors created when open. She'd laugh and squeal as she ran in one set of doors, passing through the living room, entry hall and dining room, before bursting out the other set of doors and arriving on the opposite end of the veranda. It had been a senseless game only a child would enjoy but the memory soothed her aching heart.

With a sigh, she opened her car door and approached the front door. She reached for the door knob, then dropped her hand, unsure if she should walk in unannounced. Theoretically it *was* still her home, she reminded herself. But her father's house-keeper lived there and Gina thought it best not to startle the woman unnecessarily.

With that in mind, she pressed the doorbell. Moments later the door opened and a gray-haired woman appeared. She looked at Gina in puzzlement. "May I help you?"

Gina took an uneasy step back, thinking she'd made a mistake in coming. "I'm sorry. I probably should've called first."

The woman's eyes flared in recognition. "Gina!" she cried, then caught Gina's hand and tugged her inside. "Don't be ridiculous," she fussed. "There's no need for you to ever call. This is your home."

Gina allowed herself to be drawn inside. "I don't know why I came," she said helplessly. "I left the lawyer's office, intending to go home."

The housekeeper's face softened in compassion. "You are home, dear."

Gina fought back tears. "Thank you. I just want to look around a minute, if that's okay."

The housekeeper nodded sympathetically, as if understanding Gina's need to reconnect with her past. "Of course it's okay, dear. If you need anything, I'll be in the kitchen."

Gina watched the housekeeper disappear down the hall, then turned a slow circle, taking in the familiar sights of the home she'd grown up in. The oil portrait of her mother still hung over the fireplace, and the same family photos framed in silver stood on the mantle. Feeling as if nothing had changed in the twelve years since she'd last been home, Gina walked down the hall and stopped in front of the study.

Paneled in a rich walnut, the room had served as her father's home office and appeared to still serve that purpose. His desk sat in the center of the room, the leather chair behind it angled slightly, as if he'd just pushed away from his work and was planning to return. To the left of the desktop sat his pipe stand and the humidor that held his tobacco. She inhaled deeply, filling her senses with the aromatic scent that lingered in the air.

Growing bolder, she crossed the room and sat in his chair. She spun slowly around, taking in all the familiar objects in the room. The antique hat stand beside the door. The built-in bookshelves filled with books and what-nots he'd collected over the years. The windows that looked over the rose garden. As the chair slowly stopped to face the desk again, her gaze settled on a picture frame placed on the desktop at her right. Numbed by the sight, she reached to pick up the frame and stared at the collage of images beneath the glass. Photos of her as a baby, a toddler, one of her school pictures. First grade or second. She couldn't remember which.

But the most shocking was the newspaper clipping that partially covered a few of the photos. Yellowed with age, the article was the one that had appeared in her college newspaper, announcing the sale of her first book. She stared at the clipping, wondering how he'd obtained it and, more, why he'd kept it all these years.

She stood slowly to replace the frame, then rounded the desk and continued her tour, emotion filling her throat. At the door of her parents' room, she stopped and drew in a bracing breath. It was then that she smelt it. The unmistakable scent of decay associated with a cancer patient. Though faint, the scent remained as a reminder of the man who had battled the illness.

The tears surged higher and she made herself take that first frightening step inside her father's room, the one in which he'd drawn his last breath. Though she'd been told he'd spent his last days in this room, no medical paraphernalia remained to indicate the battle he'd waged against the disease that had ultimately taken his life. The bed was neatly made, the drapes pulled back to let in the bright sunshine. A vase of blooms from the rose garden sat on the bedside table. Two framed pictures graced the table as well.

Not remembering the pictures having been there in her youth, Gina moved closer to study them. She gulped back tears, when she saw that one contained a photo of her mother, the other a snapshot of herself. He *had* loved them, she realized slowly. Though he'd never understood how to show his love for his family, the feelings had obviously been there and remained even after his wife and daughter were no longer a part of his life.

Gina drove back to her loft on autopilot, totally unaware of her surroundings or really where she was going. Though her heart was still heavy with regret, it had been warmed by the discoveries she'd made at her father's house.

But as she drew near downtown and her loft, that warmth gave way to the chilling realization of what Case had done, how he'd used her.

When she stepped off the elevator, she turned for Zoie's loft, rather than her own, wanting to avoid the memories of Case her loft held. Finding the door locked, she called, "Zoie? It's me. Gina. I don't have my key."

She started to raise her fist to knock, then dropped it, with a moan, remembering that Zoie had left that morning to visit Sulley. Her steps leaden, she walked back down the hall to her loft.

Once inside, she stripped off her coat and hung it in the closet, then crossed to her bedroom, not daring to look either left or right for fear of seeing something that would remind of her of Case. One of his ties draped over the back of a chair; a shoe peeking out from beneath the sofa; the newspaper he'd read while eating breakfast.

She'd made the bed before leaving that morning and, as was her habit, placed Timothy Toad in his position of honor on top of her pillow. The sight of the stuffed animal nearly dragged her to her knees. With tears filling her eyes, she picked the toad up and sank down, burying her face in his soft green fur. Until she'd read her father's letter, she'd forgotten that he had given her Timothy Toad. Or maybe she'd blocked the memory from her mind, the same as she'd blocked her father from her life.

She allowed the memory to return, recalling the events surrounding the gift. Her father had missed her eighth birthday party, because of an out-of-town business trip he'd sworn he couldn't miss. While away, he'd bought the toad and given it to her upon his return. Gina had treasured the gift, sure that it was a sign her father was thinking about her, even when he was away. Her mother had burst her bubble by reminding Gina that showering them with gifts was his way of making up for his absence.

With a sigh, she hugged the toad to her waist. Whatever his reason, all these years later her father had remembered giving her the gift and that meant more to her than the gift itself.

As she sat holding the toad, fresh tears welled in her eyes, as her mind segued to Case and her finding his name on the legal documents at the lawyer's office. He'd lied to her. Used her. And, like a fool, she'd let herself be snookered by his handsome face and pretty words.

What was she going to do? she asked herself miserably. Should she confront him with her suspicions? Demand he tell her why he had never mentioned the merger? Why the date of the merger coincided with the day their engagement was announced in the newspaper?

He'd sworn he didn't know who had leaked the news to the press, but she had to believe that he'd lied about that, too. He was the only person who had stood to benefit from the leak, as it was the perfect means to let her father know about the engagement.

It all made so much sense now, each of his moves crystal clear. He had never been interested in her romantically. From the moment he'd appeared at her booksigning, his one and only goal had been obtaining Reynolds Refining.

She pressed a hand over her heart, the pain that realization drew striking sharp and deep. She didn't want to believe she'd fallen in love with a man who could be so cruel, so cold-bloodedly ruthless, but it appeared she had little choice. What other explanation could there be for his behavior?

She thought back over the previous month, since meeting Case, evaluating each time they'd been together, his actions, things he'd said. A hollow feeling opened in her stomach as she remembered he'd never once said he loved her. And the one time she'd asked him specifically if he did, he'd avoided responding by asking a question instead. He'd done that a lot. Answering a question with a question. A non-answer, Gina realized now, as that hollow spot in her stomach grew wider. Politicians did it all the time, in order to avoid a subject they preferred not to discuss.

Let's not worry about that right now. We'll plan on having a long engagement. As long as you want.

Anger burned through her as she remembered how he'd responded to her request to elope. He'd never intended to marry her. From day one, the whole engagement had been a farce designed to fool her father into believing that, as Case's wife, she would receive the legacy he wanted for her. Everything Case had said to her, everything he'd done, had all been a well-choreographed act, a devious plan to gain control of Reynolds Refining.

Even making love to her.

And that hurt more than anything. That he would use an act of love for selfish gain both sickened and destroyed her. She had given him her virginity, bared her soul, her very heart to him. And for what?

The acquisition of a corporation.

* * *

Case glanced at the clock on the wall of his office and frowned when he saw that it was after twelve-thirty. Concerned that Gina hadn't called yet, he picked up the phone and punched in the attorney's number.

"Cravens, Conners and O'Reilly. How may I direct your call?"

Having spent a great deal of time in Cravens' office while working on the merger, Case recognized the voice of the receptionist who answered. "Hey, Margo. Case Fortune. Is Gina still there with Cravens?"

"No, Mr. Fortune. She left hours ago. She became ill while she was here and asked Mr. Cravens if they could reschedule."

Frowning, Case thanked Margo and disconnected the call. *Ill?* Gina hadn't mentioned feeling ill when she'd left that morning. Nervous, yes, but not ill.

"Oh, God," he moaned and dropped his head to his hands, realizing what had made her sick. She knew. Somehow Gina had found out about the merger. When she'd first told Case about the appointment with Cravens, she'd said that it was a preliminary meeting, an opportunity for Cravens to familiarize Gina with her father's personal finances. Case had assumed that meant his home, utilities, his personal bank accounts. He'd never dreamed that Cravens would address Reynolds Refining.

And now she knew everything. How Case had deceived her. How he'd used her as a pawn in his game to get control of her father's company.

Groaning, he dropped his face to his hands. He'd never meant to hurt her. But that's exactly what he'd done. And now he was going to lose her. His own greed was going to rob him of the woman he loved.

He dropped his hands and bolted from his desk. He had to talk to her, he thought desperately. He'd explain everything. Confess his every sin. She'd understand. She had to.

Fifteen minutes later, Case was stepping off the elevator and approaching Gina's door. Finding it locked, he automatically reached in his pocket for the key she'd given him…then slowly withdrew his hand. For some reason, he didn't feel it was right to use the key. Not when she knew now what he'd done.

Instead, he knocked, waited, then knocked again. When she didn't answer, he called, "Gina? It's me. Case." He waited, listening, but didn't hear a sound from within. She was home, he thought in frustration. He knew she was. He'd seen her car in the garage only minutes ago when he parked there himself.

"Gina, please," he begged. "I can explain."

Again, only silence. He considered using the key again, then turned away, knowing he didn't deserve the trust she'd honored him with in giving him the key. He'd betrayed her. Used her.

Swallowing back the fear that tightened his chest, he punched the elevator button that would take him to the garage. He had to do something, he told himself. He couldn't lose Gina. Not when he'd fallen in love with her. There had to be a way he could prove to her that he loved her, that it was her he wanted and not her father's company.

Eight

"Gina?" Zoie called, as she stepped into the loft.

"In here," Gina called then quickly blotted her eyes and cheeks. She might be a wreck, she told herself, but that didn't mean she had to look the part.

Zoie rounded the privacy screen that separated Gina's bedroom from the rest of the loft and immediately slammed to a stop. "Whoa," she said, staring. "What happened to you? Did somebody else die?"

Gina's face crumpled. "No, but I wish *I* had," she sobbed miserably.

Zoie fisted her hands on her hips. "That's crazy talk and you better stop it right now."

Gina dabbed at her nose. "I know. I'm sorry. I didn't mean it. Not literally, anyway."

Her face softening in compassion, Zoie sank down on the bed beside Gina and draped an arm around her shoulders. "What's wrong, honey? Why are you crying?"

Gina sniffed. "Case lied. He really never intended to marry me."

Zoie's eyebrows shot up in surprise. "He broke your engagement? Oh, honey, I'm so sorry."

Gina shook her head. "No. No. He didn't break the engagement. He didn't have to. It was all a farce. From the beginning. A way for him to get control of my father's company."

Zoie looked at her in puzzlement. "But he gave you a ring. A *big* ring. And it was announced in the paper."

"All of it was a lie, a part of his plan. He wanted to merge Reynolds Refining with Dakota Fortunes. Initially my father agreed, but backed out on the deal when he found out he had cancer. He wanted to leave the company to me, as a legacy, instead."

"Oh, Gina," Zoie moaned softly, "that's so sweet. I mean about your father wanting the leaving the company to you," she clarified quickly. "Not about Case lying."

"He wrote me a letter. Dad did. His lawyer gave it to me this morning. In it he said the rift in our relationship was his fault, that he loved me and always had. And he said that he wished he had lived long enough to see Case and me marry, to hold the children we would have some day."

"Oh, Gina, honey," Zoie said with regret.

Gina nodded miserably. "I know. Think of all the years we wasted." She drew in a ragged breath, released it. "But at least I know now he cared." She set her jaw, her mind segueing to Case. "That's more than I can say for Case."

"Are you sure about all this?" Zoie asked doubtfully. "About Case, I mean."

Gina sniffed. "Positive. I saw the documents for the merger at the lawyer's office. When Dad backed out of the deal, Case's only option to get hold of Reynolds Refining was to marry me."

"Have you talked to him about it? I mean, the evidence is damning and all that, but maybe there's another explanation."

Gina dropped her chin and shook her head. "He came by earlier, but I wouldn't answer the door."

"Gina!" Zoie cried. "You should at least give him the opportunity to explain."

"And listen to another lie?" Gina adamantly shook her head. "No, thanks. I've listened to enough of his lies."

Zoie jutted her chin. "Well, I refuse to believe Case would do anything so low. I *saw* the two of you together! How he looked at you, the way he hovered over you during your father's funeral. That was *real,* Gina. A man can't fake those kind of emotions."

"Obviously Case can."

Gina hadn't slept a wink all night. She'd tossed and turned, cried some more and basically held her own private pity party. When she finally crawled from bed, she was bleary-eyed and felt a headache threatening.

Forcing herself to follow her normal routine, she made a cup of coffee, popped a frozen cinnamon roll into the microwave, then sat down at the table to eat. The phone rang. She considered ignoring it, but her curiosity got the better of her and she rose to check Caller ID. Seeing the name and number of Mr. Cravens' law office, she hesitated a moment, then picked up the phone.

"Hello?"

"Good morning, Gina," Cravens said. "I apologize for calling so early, but I felt this couldn't wait. I received a phone call from Case last night."

She flattened her lips, wishing now that she hadn't answered the phone. "I'm really not interested in anything Case has to say."

"You'll want to hear this," Cravens warned.

Gina frowned at the graveness of Craven's tone. "Is there a problem?"

"You could say so," he said, and she was surprised to hear the spike of anger in his voice. "Case has withdrawn Dakota Fortunes' offer to purchase Reynolds Refining."

Stunned, for a moment Gina could only stare. "But…why?"

"He didn't offer a reason. I reminded him that Dakota Fortunes will forfeit all monies invested to this point, which are considerable, I might add, and he said that Dakota Fortunes wouldn't lose anything on the deal, as he plans to personally assume responsibility for the debt."

For Case to absorb the loss didn't make sense to Gina. But she quickly shoved the thought away, focusing instead on how this unexpected change of plans would affect her. "So what happens now?" she asked uncertainly.

"You'll have to take over the management of Reynolds Refining."

Gina's jaw dropped. "But I don't know anything about running a company!"

"You better learn," he warned. "Curtis has an excellent management team in place, but without someone present with the authority to make decisions, the company will go belly up in less than six months. Competitors have already heard of Curtis's death and are circling like vultures."

Gina pressed a hand to the headache that was now throbbing between her eyes. "I need time to think," she said wearily. "This is too much to take in at one time."

Promising to call later in the day, she hung up the phone and returned to her chair at the table. Why was Case doing this? she asked herself in frustration. Did he think that by withdrawing Dakota Fortunes' offer to purchase Reynolds Refining he could purchase it later for a bargain price? He knew she didn't want the company and knew she lacked the skills to successfully manage it.

Anger burned through her. It was one thing to play with Gina's emotions, but to purposefully sabotage her father's company was downright mean!

She heard the scrape of a key in the lock and tensed, thinking it might be Case. She heaved a sigh of relief when the door swung open and she saw that it was Zoie. Her relief quickly gave way to annoyance when she saw that Zoie's face was flushed with anger, the same as it had been the night before when Zoie had left.

"If you think you can browbeat me into talking to Case," she warned, "forget it. I have even more reason to distrust him now. I just spoke to Dad's attorney. He called to tell me Case has withdrawn Dakota Fortune's offer to purchase Reynolds Refining, which means that now I have to take over managing the company."

"The snake," Zoie said, with a snarl. "And here

I thought he couldn't stoop any lower than he already had."

Gina frowned, confused by the sudden change in Zoie's opinion of Case. "What do you mean, worse?"

"Brace yourself," Zoie warned as she tossed a newspaper in front of Gina. "This is ugly."

Her stomach knotting in dread, Gina opened the paper and found herself looking at a photograph of Case. Below it, the heading Merger Of Fortunes—Nixed.

She read the first sentence of the accompanying article, then stopped and read it again.

Late last night, Case Fortune announced the end of his engagement to Gina Reynolds, heiress to Curtis Reynolds' estate.

"The nerve of the jerk!" Zoie cried, waving a hand at the headline. "He's not only a heartless bastard, he's a cowardly one, at that. He could've just told you he wanted to break off the engagement, but, oh no," she said bitterly, "he has to plaster it all over the newspaper for the whole world to see."

"He did try to talk to me yesterday," Gina admitted reluctantly. "But I refused to answer the door."

Zoie humphed. "Like any woman in her right mind would throw out the welcome mat to a snake like him."

As Gina continued to stare at the picture of Case before her, anger built inside her until she felt as if she was going to choke on it. Setting her jaw, she snatched up the newspaper and marched to the closet.

"Where are you going?" Zoie cried in dismay.

"To talk to Case," Gina said, shrugging on her coat.

"You're going to tell him off?" Zoie asked hopefully.

"You're darn right, I am," Gina said furiously. "I've been a bystander in my own life long enough. It's time I took a stand."

Zoie shot to her feet. "Can I go and watch?"

Gina jerked open the door. "Not this time," she muttered darkly. "I'm doing this alone."

Gina drove straight to the Dakota Fortunes' building, confident that she'd find Case in his office, his attitude one of business as usual. Why should this day be any different? she asked herself. No one had screwed with his life, the way Case had screwed with hers.

Without a thought to the odd glances she received, she strode straight for Case's office.

Case's secretary looked up from her computer monitor, her eyes widening when she saw Gina. "Ms. Reynolds," she said in surprise. "You're wearing a nightgown."

Gina glanced down and saw the hem of her nightgown peeking from beneath her coat and scowled. "So what if I am?" she returned irritably. "Is Case in his office?"

Marcia cast a worried glanced over her shoulder at the door behind her. "Uh…yes, ma'am, he is." She glanced back at Gina. "Would you like for me to tell him you're here?"

Gina swept past Marcia, her nose in the air. "That won't be necessary. I'll tell him myself."

She opened the door, then sank back against it, turning the lock as she closed the door behind her. She wasn't sure if she was locking the door to prevent anyone from interrupting her conversation with Case, or to keep herself from bolting out, should she lose her nerve.

He glanced up and his eyes shot wide in surprise. "Gina."

Though her knees quaked uncontrollably, she managed to keep her voice steady. "Good morning, Case," she said coolly.

He rose slowly. "What are you doing here?"

"Mr. Cravens called this morning to tell me you've withdrawn your offer to purchase Reynold's Refining."

He nodded. "That's true. I have."

It angered her even more that he appeared to feel no shame for his deceit. Determined to make him crawl before she was done, she pushed away from the door and moved to stand opposite his desk. "I have to be honest," she said, secretly proud of the indifference she kept in her tone. "At first I thought you'd done it in hopes of snapping up Reynolds Refining later for a bargain price."

"No," he said, shaking his head. "That wasn't my purpose, though I'm not surprised you'd think such a thing of me."

Was that a little admission of guilt? she wondered. Regret? She quickly shoved the notion aside, deciding it didn't matter. Not any longer.

"Zoie dropped by this morning," she went on conversationally. "She showed me the article in the paper, where you'd officially announced the end of our engagement."

"I tried to talk to you yesterday. I wanted to explain, but—"

"My fault," she said, holding up a hand. "I didn't want to talk to you then. I was upset. Understandably so," she added, her smile saccharine sweet. "It came as quite a shock to discover your plans to merge Reynolds Refining with Dakota Fortunes. Odd, isn't it, that you never once mentioned your plans to me?"

He had the grace to blush, which pleased her enormously.

She tipped her head and looked at him curiously. "Tell me something, Case. Was obtaining Reynolds Refining really worth marrying a woman you didn't love?"

A muscle ticked on his jaw. "I never thought it would go that far," he snapped.

Gina had gone to his office to force him to admit to what he'd done to her, how he'd used her. But she hadn't realized that hearing him confess to his guilt would hurt as much as it did. That hurt must have registered on her face, because Case dropped his face to his hands with a groan.

"I'm sorry. I didn't mean that the way it sounded."

She jutted her chin. "No, I'm sure you didn't." She twisted the engagement from her finger and held it out to him. "Hopefully you can return this and get your money back."

He lifted his head and Gina was shocked at the misery she saw in his eyes.

"I don't want the ring, Gina. I bought it for you."

She thrust the ring at him, determined not to let him fool her again. "For all the wrong reasons," she reminded him.

Heaving a sigh, he took the ring and stared down at it. "I'm sorry, Gina. I never meant to hurt you."

She lifted a brow. "Really? And how did you plan to avoid that? Women take proposals very seriously. Most of us consider it a profession of love, a promise of a lifelong commitment."

He hung his head. "And it should be." He lifted his head and, for a second time, she had to remind herself that the misery his face revealed was nothing more than an act.

"I was wrong, Gina," he said quietly. "So wrong to do what I did to you. I wanted your father's company and you were the only means available to me to get it. Without any consideration for you or your feelings, I decided to use you as a bargaining tool."

Gina had heard enough. If she listened to another word, she feared her heart would break completely in two. How could she have fallen in love with a man who was so cold-hearted? So ruthless? How could she still love him, after all he'd done? But she did love him, which was why she had to leave. She'd die before she'd let him know she was that foolish, that stupid.

"If you're asking for forgiveness," she told him, "you might want to talk to a priest. You certainly won't receive it from me." With that, she turned for the door. She had her hand on the knob, when his voice stopped her.

"Gina. Wait. Please."

She wouldn't listen to any more, couldn't. She tried to open the lock, but tears blinded her, making her fingers fumble on the mechanism.

Before she could twist it open, his hand lit on her shoulder and she tensed beneath the weight.

"Gina," he said softly and turned her to face him.

She blinked the tears back, not wanting him to see how much he'd hurt her.

"If you're wanting to know my plans for Reynolds Refining," she informed him, "I'm not keeping it. I never wanted the company and wouldn't know what to do with it, even if I did."

"But Curtis wanted you to have it. It was his legacy for you."

"The only legacy I ever wanted from my father was his love. I discovered in a letter he left for me that I'd had it all along." She dropped her gaze, knowing in her heart that's what she'd wanted from Case. His love. "But I doubt you would understand the value I place in that single word."

"Oh, but I do." He placed a knuckle beneath her chin and forced her face up until her gaze met his. "Yesterday morning, as you were leaving to meet Cravens, you said you loved me."

"Did I?" she replied flippantly. "I don't recall saying that."

"Trust me, you did." He dropped his hand and moved closer, until his face was only inches from hers. "What I want to know is, do you still?"

She wanted to laugh in his face, lie and tell him that they were only words, she hadn't meant them. But she couldn't lie, as he'd lied to her. Foolish or not, her emotions, were not something she could control. She did love him, and feared she would until the day she died.

But she wasn't a doormat, a woman to be walked on or pitied for giving her heart to the wrong man. Setting her jaw, she shoved his hand away and turned for the door again. "Don't worry. I'll get over it."

"Please don't."

Her fingers froze on the lock.

He placed his hands on her shoulders, squeezed. "I love you, Gina. My intentions may have been dishonest in the beginning, but they aren't now. Haven't been for weeks. I fell in love with you, without even realizing it. But trust me when I say I fell hard. Marry me, Gina. Today, tomorrow, next year. I don't care when. Just promise that you won't ever stop loving me."

She turned slowly to peer at him, sure that this was another act, a ploy to trick her. "Case…"

When he lowered his face, as if he were going to kiss her, she pressed her fingers against his lips, blocking him. "I need to know. Why did you withdraw your offer to buy Reynolds Refining?"

He drew her fingers from his mouth and squeezed them tightly, as if desperate to make her believe him. "Because I knew when you refused to talk to me yesterday, that you'd found out about the merger and would think that was the reason I had proposed."

"But it *was*!" she cried. "You said so yourself."

"In the beginning, yes. But not now. I fell in love

with you, Gina. That wasn't part of my plan, I assure you. But you mean more to me than anything ever will."

Though she wanted to believe him, she didn't dare allow herself to until he'd absolved every doubt. "If that's true, why did you announce in the newspaper the end of our engagement?"

"Because I was afraid you'd think I only wanted to marry you to get control of your father's business. By withdrawing my offer for the company, as well as my proposal, I had hoped to prove that it's *you* I want, not Reynolds Refining."

She searched his eyes for any sign that he might be lying. But all she found was the warmth of his love, a sincerity that touched her heart. "Do you mean it?" she asked, not daring to hope. "If I were to tell you that I'd give you Reynolds Refining, sign it over to you without any strings attached, would you still want to marry me?"

A soft smile pulled at one corner of his mouth as he tucked a strand of hair behind her ear. "You can close the doors on the company, sell it to the highest bidder, for all I care. What I want is *you*. I love you, Gina. More than I can ever express."

She released a long breath, too stunned to form any kind of response. "Oh, Case."

"Does that mean you'll marry me?" he asked hopefully.

Laughing, she threw her arms around his neck. "Yes, I'll marry you! Today, tomorrow, next year. I don't care when. Just promise that you won't ever stop loving me."

"Hey," he cried, pretending indignation. "That was my line."

Smiling, she drew back to frame his face between her hands. "So sue me. Can I help it if I feel the same way?"

He drew her hips firmly against his. "Tell me you love me."

"I love you."

"Tell me you'll love me forever."

"I'll love you forever."

"Tell me you love me more than you do Timothy Toad."

When she hesitated, Case choked a breath. "You love that toad more than you love me?"

"I didn't say that."

"No," he replied. "You didn't say anything at all."

She winced. "It's not that I love him more," she said carefully. "I've just loved him longer."

He narrowed an eye. "What's the life expectancy for a toad?"

She blinked, then laughed. "For heaven's sake, Case. He's a stuffed toad!"

"Maybe so, but I won't have the woman I love, loving a toad more than she does me."

Hiding a smile, she walked her fingers up his chest. "How could I love Timothy Toad more, when there are things you can do for me that he can't."

"Like that?"

"Like this," she said, and pressed her lips to his.

Humming his pleasure, he held her hips against his and rocked his groin against hers. "Yeah," he murmured against her lips. "Like that."

The telephone on his desk rang.

"Aren't you going to get that?" she asked.

He reached behind him, picked up the receiver, dropped it on his desk, then found her mouth again. "Now where were we?" he murmured huskily.

"Case!" she whispered frantically, trying to wriggle free. "Whoever's on the phone might hear us!"

"So what if they do? It's not against the law for a man to kiss his fianceé."

He used his mouth, his hands to distract her from her concerns about the phone and the person on the other end of the line. He was good with both, she thought with a shiver. Damned good.

When at last he withdrew, it was only far enough to nuzzle her neck with his nose.

"Case?" she asked hesitantly.

"Hmm?"

"Are we going to live at your family's estate when we get married?"

He drew back with a frown. "Would you mind, if we did?"

She wrinkled her nose. "Well, yeah, sort of. It's not that I don't like your family," she hurried to assure him, then dropped her gaze, blushing. "It's just…well, so…crowded there. People running in and out all the time. What if someone were to come in our room, while we were…well, you know."

He dropped his head back and laughed. "Gina, Gina, Gina," he chided. "No one will come into our suite, unless they're invited."

"Well, they might," she insisted stubbornly.

Smiling, he bumped his nose against hers. "We don't have to live there. We can live anywhere you want. Your loft. My suite here at Dakota Fortunes. Or we can build a house. The choice is yours."

"You mean it?" she asked in excitement. "You'd really let me choose where we're going to live?"

"Yes, I mean it." He placed a knuckle beneath her chin and held her face before his. "As long as you're with me, I don't care where we live."

"Oh, Case," she cried, flinging her arms around him and hugging him tight. "I never dreamed I could ever be this happy."

"Me, either, Gina," he said with a contented sigh. "Me, either."

* * * * *

The DAKOTA FORTUNES *series*
continues next month with
BACK IN FORTUNE'S BED
by Bronwyn Jameson

Happily ever after is just the beginning…

Turn the page for a sneak preview of
DANCING ON SUNDAY AFTERNOONS
by
Linda Cardillo

Harlequin Everlasting—Every great love
has a story to tell.™
A brand-new line from Harlequin Books
launching this February!

Prologue

Giulia D'Orazio
1983

I had two husbands—Paolo and Salvatore.

Salvatore and I were married for thirty-two years. I still live in the house he bought for us; I still sleep in our bed. All around me are the signs of our life together. My bedroom window looks out over the garden he planted. In the middle of the city, he coaxed tomatoes, peppers, zucchini—even grapes for his wine—out of the ground. On weekends, he used to drive up to his cousin's farm in Waterbury and bring back manure. In the winter, he wrapped the peach tree and the fig tree with rags and black rubber hoses against the cold, his massive, coarse hands gentling those trees as if they were his fragile-skinned babies.

My neighbor, Dominic Grazza, does that for me now. My boys have no time for the garden.

In the front of the house, Salvatore planted roses. The roses I take care of myself. They are giant, cream-colored, fragrant. In the afternoons, I like to sit out on the porch with my coffee, protected from the eyes of the neighborhood by that curtain of flowers.

Salvatore died in this house thirty-five years ago. In the last months, he lay on the sofa in the parlor so he could be in the middle of everything. Except for the two oldest boys, all the children were still at home and we ate together every evening. Salvatore could see the dining room table from the sofa, and he could hear everything that was said. "I'm not dead, yet," he told me. "I want to know what's going on."

When my first grandchild, Cara, was born, we brought her to him, and he held her on his chest, stroking her tiny head. Sometimes they fell asleep together.

Over on the radiator cover in the corner of the parlor is the portrait Salvatore and I had taken on our twenty-fifth anniversary. This brooch I'm wearing today, with the diamonds—I'm wearing it in the photograph also—Salvatore gave it to me that day. Upstairs on my dresser is a jewelry box filled with necklaces and bracelets and earrings. All from Salvatore.

I am surrounded by the things Salvatore gave

me, or did for me. But, God forgive me, as I lie alone now in my bed, it is Paolo I remember.

Paolo left me nothing. Nothing, that is, that my family, especially my sisters, thought had any value. No house. No diamonds. Not even a photograph.

But after he was gone, and I could catch my breath from the pain, I knew that I still had something. In the middle of the night, I sat alone and held them in my hands, reading the words over and over until I heard his voice in my head. I had Paolo's letters.

* * * * *

REQUEST YOUR FREE BOOKS!

2 FREE NOVELS PLUS 2 FREE GIFTS!

 Silhouette® Desire®

Passionate, Powerful, Provocative!

SDES06

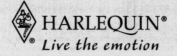

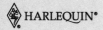

HARLEQUIN®

E V E R L A S T I N G   L O V E™

Every great love has a story to tell™

Save $1.⁰⁰ off

**the purchase of
any Harlequin
Everlasting Love novel**

Coupon valid from January 1, 2007
until April 30, 2007.

**Valid at retail outlets in the U.S. only.
Limit one coupon per customer.**

5 65373 00076 2   (8100) 0 11302

HEUSCPN0407

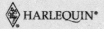

HARLEQUIN®

EVERLASTING LOVE™

Every great love has a story to tell™

Fall from Grace

Kristi Gold

Save $1.⁰⁰ off

the purchase of
any Harlequin
Everlasting Love novel

Coupon valid from January 1, 2007
until April 30, 2007.

Valid at retail outlets in Canada only.
Limit one coupon per customer.

52607370

HECDNCPN0407

HARLEQUIN® *Romance*®

What a month!

In February watch for

Rancher and Protector
Part of the Western Weddings miniseries
BY JUDY CHRISTENBERRY

The Boss's Pregnancy Proposal
BY RAYE MORGAN

Also in February, expect
MORE of what you love
as the Harlequin Romance line
increases to six titles per month.